A PATRIOT FOR IVANOV

A PATRIOT FOR IVANOV

C.L. MCGINNIS

A PERMUTED PRESS BOOK
ISBN: 979-8-89565-597-9
ISBN (eBook): 979-8-89565-598-6

A Patriot for Ivanov

Cover Design by Jim Villaflores

Permuted Press
New York • Nashville
permutedpress.com

Published in the United States of America
1 2 3 4 5 6 7 8 9 10

DEDICATION

For

Mrs. Moyers and all the other English teachers attempting to salvage the adolescent mind.

And for

Independence 08. We shall never forget.

CHAPTER 1

2011. Helmand Province, Afghanistan. 1300 Zulu.

To be a creature of habit is to have a pattern of life. To be studied. To be capable of being studied, even from eight thousand feet above, via a small twin-engine turboprop plane and an aircrew of four men in nondescript tan flight suits, all of whom woke up one morning with the intention of ruining your day. There is a kind of intimacy behind their killing, to know the minute details of a target's gait, his lean on a motorbike, the way his family greets him, his comfort with the Kalashnikov that hangs over his right shoulder.

The plane is small. A C-12 filled with stacks of seemingly innocuous electrical boxes, knobs and switches, levers that could start the wrong war if left in the wrong hands. In the back of the plane, with headset on and eyes scanning multiple computer monitors, sits Logan Callahan, a late-twenties attractive airman with a chiseled face and average height. He has the physique of a runner but a studious gaze that might suggest he is more comfortable in a library than a gymnasium. He addresses the flight crew through his headset.

"Pilot, C.O., need to get below these clouds, request flight level 070."

The first of two pilots on board responds.

"Roger C.O. Let's see what they can give us."

A moment passes as the pilot confirms the request with an unheard air traffic controller. The pilot breaks the silence again.

"Crew, Pilot. Moving to flight level 070."

"Copy, thank you," replies Logan.

The small plane drops in altitude to seven thousand feet as the aircrew watches the monitors. Out of a small window near his head, Logan can see the jagged peaks of mountains scattered throughout Helmand, emerging from the dusty ground as ancient teeth in a Martian landscape.

At the base of these mountains sits a small hut occupied by an Afghan male in his forties. His Pashtun garb, untrimmed beard, and karakul hat are just as weathered as the hut itself, as if the man is merely an extension of that particular arid patch of terrain. The man exits from the hut, walking twenty feet toward a motorbike propped against a large boulder. Perhaps out of curiosity or hubris, he pauses to look up toward the sky, as if to acknowledge the sound of the plane circling overhead.

At seven thousand feet above, Logan addresses the crew.

"Crew, C.O., have visual on one military-aged male approaching motorbike."

The second pilot responds.

"C.O., Pilot, confirm eyes on HVT?"

"Unknown if this is our guy. Standby one," answers Logan.

The silence among the aircrew is intense while they wait for Logan to methodically perform his magic, oscillating between stern glances at multiple computer monitors and typing messages to an unknown intelligence customer thousands of miles away. One monitor portrays on overhead real-time view of the Afghan male approaching the motorbike down below.

A bead of sweat forms on Logan's brow. He is aware of the urgency of the moment, but he has his method, and his method works.

The second pilot disrupts the moment. "C.O., Pilot, JSOC is asking if this is our guy."

"Standby," responds Logan.

Logan's response is curt and unsatisfactory for the increasingly overzealous crew. Some want blood. Some want accolades from the special operations community monitoring their mission. And some just want to return back to the Kandahar chow hall in time for chicken fingers Friday.

A third crew member chimes in.

"C.O. we gotta make a call. We're gonna lose him!"

A monitor in front of Logan displays the weathered Afghan male pulling his motorbike off the boulder and beginning to climb on. Logan has all the information he needs to make the call.

"I'm calling it. Confirmation. Positive ID. JSOC aware at this time. Standby for strike."

In a nearby airspace, an unmanned aerial vehicle circles, adjusts, and prepares to rain hell from above, while thousands of feet below, the target of Logan's focus starts up his motorbike, unknowingly preparing to have his final ride into the Afghanistan sunset. Suddenly a cacophony of flame, twisted metal, and shrapnel can be heard throughout the valley. Smoke, dirt, and debris cloud the air where the motorbike had been.

Logan watches through a monitor as the smoke begins to clear, revealing the mutilated body of his target, writhing around in the dirt, grasping for life. His limbs are held together just enough to be recognizable as a mangled human. His hands attempt to cup his protruding intestines, like a surreal form of puppetry unfolding on a charred dirt floor. Suddenly two women in Afghan garb, along with three adolescent children, emerge from the target's hut, running toward the squirming remains of their father and husband. They quickly pick up what is left of his body and place it in a white sheet, scurrying off with the body to some unknown destination.

Logan remains silent as the other crew members cheer loudly, high-fiving. He watches and waits. The enemy is resilient. Logan never celebrates victory prematurely. He never celebrates at all.

* * *

Back at his squadron in Kandahar, Logan Callahan is standing in a hallway next to an open locker, pulling various items out of the pockets of his flight suit and placing them inside. As he proceeds with this post-mission ritual, he hears the familiar footsteps of his friend John approaching around the corner. John is slightly taller than Logan, with a bigger build and buzzed blond hair. His flight suit is multiple shades of tan, owing largely to the lack of prioritization he places upon personal hygiene in the deployed environment. He is affable, but only as long as his minimal frustration tolerance can allow.

And he is often frustrated, but rarely ever with Logan. The two men exchange greetings.

"I heard you guys got him. Awesome," says John. "You been watching that dude for like three months, right? Crazy. Anyway man, some mail came for you."

Logan's expression is neutral, a quiet reservation as he extends his hand to collect a small, white, rectangular envelope from his friend. Mail can be a welcome sight in this hellscape.

Most letters are predictably from family and friends. Occasionally a group of schoolchildren might send a card or care package, thanking a military member for their service and simultaneously reminding that folks at home still believe there's something glamorous about all of it. But this letter is different, and Logan's trepidation is both palpable and understandable to John. This is a piece of mail that will dictate Logan's future. Will he soon be off to graduate school in Washington, DC? Or will he be destined to slogging out a life as a defense contractor when his military service ends in a few months? The letter is from George Washington University. He opens the contents slowly.

"Time to make it or break it," Logan mumbles.

He grips the letter firmly, reading silently. His expression changes, and a rare smile forms on his face as he lifts his gaze to meet the eyes of his curious friend.

Enthusiastically, Logan announces, "Well dude, maybe it's finally happening. I got in!"

School had never been particularly challenging for Logan, not academically anyway. He had the gift of learning a subject overnight, if the fervor was necessitated, such as it typically was during the final night before an exam. He did his best never to waste anyone's money, especially his own. If his cognitive capacities were ever under scrutiny, he excelled. He placed tremendous emphasis on conviction and accountability, although only as far as meeting the expectations of others. Sleep deprivation and excessive caffeine intake were of little consequence in his youth.

Born and raised in the industrial Midwest, he grew up working with his hands. Manual labor had been the norm, and college, for most, was just a fantasy. Logan had been in the unfortunate position of being a brilliant kid in a region of the country that valued street smarts and frowned upon his idiosyncrasies. So he learned to adapt and pursued interests on his own time, when no one was looking. In the evenings he would drive into the city for boxing lessons. On his drive home he would listen to Miles Davis and silently pontificate on the intricacies of "Flamenco Sketches." During the school day he would sneak away and smoke cigarettes behind the gas station. He became sexually active before the other boys but told no one. He was dangerously mature for an adolescent. Earning decent grades came easy for him, but navigating the interpersonal dynamics of seemingly insignificant small talk with peers felt much more taxing. So he challenged himself by learning how to adapt to demonstrably varied social climates, becoming an expert in suppressing social anxiety whenever he was under observation. He was rebellious but never could find the words to explain why. He smashed car windows and picked fights with kids twice his size. A juvenile delinquent who spent much of his youth running from the police, and never once did he get caught. He was a boy desperate for a mentor, but in such absence he settled for a beer and a blade.

In college, he took that darkness with him. He attended every class but took pride in out-drinking his peers. He paid for his textbooks with winnings from playing poker in a nearby casino. He made the dean's list but still quite frequently found himself narrowly avoiding jail. To his professors, he maintained a quiet intensity. Cerebral, yet remarkably constrained. In truth, he was often understimulated, a trait some psychiatrist in the future would one day tell him was the result of undiagnosed ADHD. Logan spent his undergraduate nights chasing women, searching for bar fights, trying to quiet a rage from a source that few would ever learn.

Logan knew the very morning of the terrorist attacks on 9/11 that he would join the military. Motivated by a desire to serve his country, a quest for revenge, and a naive wish to see war up close, he had made a promise to himself to one day walk through the doors of a recruiter's office. When he finally honored that promise after college, he sat for his initial aptitude tests, to assess, with questionable accuracy, in what capacity he might best serve the stars and stripes. Unfortunately for Logan, he scored so remarkably high on these exams that the Air Force determined he needed to become fluent in a foreign language on the government's dime. And thus, he was never quite sure whether he chose the intelligence community, or whether the intelligence community ultimately chose him. Logan outperformed his peers, often finishing training requirements weeks ahead of the scheduled curriculum. He was promoted early and celebrated as the best of the best, but he drank and he fought and he ran from the law. He was notorious for being the opposite of a team player. John, whom Logan met in basic training, largely remained his only friend.

John was a portly fellow but strangely fast on a running track. His personality could be excessively dry when sober and overly clownish when not. He was about as German as an American could be. Outside of the deployed environment, he wore glasses that were always a little too thick. It looked intentional, but there was rarely anything deliberate about his sartorial choices. He always dressed like a man thirty years older on his way to a semiformal occasion. If an event was business casual, he would show up in a suit and tie. Some could find him off-putting and aloof. But it wasn't so much that he marched to the beat of his own drum as it was that he didn't necessarily know when it was socially appropriate to have a beat at all. Some of his perceived aloofness was owed to his strict New England private school upbringing, and some of it was owed to a perpetual longing for his father's approval. In the end they were all just boys wishing they might someday make their fathers proud. Some of them were willing to go to war for it.

John came from a family of wildly successful bankers. He didn't need the military, which is exactly why he felt compelled to serve. He was searching for the one path that he was never expected to take. He would claim to regret this decision every day, except for the days when the killing happened. Someday he would probably come to regret that too. Together, Logan and John were quite the odd pairing as friends. John grew up with the silver spoon, and Logan grew up stealing it. When the opportunity to see war finally emerged for both men, they jumped and their superiors were happy to send them. And now, after experiencing the depths of humanity at its lowest, Logan was only months away from having to learn how to navigate the social intricacies of a prestigious university, all while simultaneously trying to recover from the experience of having been a government assassin, killing in the name of what some called patriotism.

CHAPTER 2

2012. George Washington University. 3:00 p.m. EST.

The basement classroom is nearly too small to contain all twenty-five of Logan's classmates. At a university notorious for its politics, foreign affairs, and legal studies, the clinical psychology doctoral program is relegated to a nondescript dusty building with poor air circulation on the far side of campus. The six figures in financial debt that would be owed upon graduation was never really payment for the education itself. It was payment for the optics of having attended *this* particular university. The White House is only blocks away. Interns on the Hill can easily move from campus to Congress. This is the ultimate breeding ground for politicians and spies, both equally treacherous.

Logan sits in the back of the classroom in a seat practically designated for quiet-mannered wallflowers. Only six months prior he had been in Afghanistan, but now, by all appearances, he was simply a perfectly average-looking graduate student. His hair was longer now and wavy, slicked back a bit. Appearing slightly older now with facial hair and the absence of a flight suit, he sports a well-trimmed beard and brown-framed glasses. Careful scrutiny might reveal a man trying a little too hard to look like an academic, but that degree of social awareness is seemingly lacking among this elite set.

The students all sit at desks with laptops open, mostly appearing to be following along to a monotonous slideshow being presented by an elderly professor next to a podium. Logan's laptop is open as well, but his attention is elsewhere, combing through international news headlines, tracking a terrorist attack somewhere in Europe, the future mining of lithium deposits in the Middle East, China's encroachment on the South China Sea. His professor's voice is merely background music for Logan's preferred pursuit of geopolitical web sleuthing.

"For those of you who will be around this weekend, I want to remind you again about a case conference that a former colleague of mine is giving at the Morgan House on intersectionality and social justice within the psychoanalytic space," mumbles the professor. "I do hope some of you will be able to attend."

The professor ends his slideshow and shuffles out of the classroom while Logan's peers begin to pack up their belongings. Logan is in no particular hurry to move from one basement classroom to the next. As he slowly begins to stand, his classmate Christie approaches, catching Logan's eye. Christie has a habit of being both awkward and attractive, a strange amalgamation of obvious athleticism and mousey appeal. She is at times sweet and flirtatious with Logan. At other moments, she can be more accurately characterized as excessively constrained. On this day, she exudes a palpable sarcasm.

"I bet you're looking forward to hitting up that case conference, aren't you?" she asks wryly.

Logan responds in kind. "Oh yeah, for sure. The last time I went to one of those, I had to listen to someone describe the significance of microaggressions in psychotherapy for two hours. Taking two hours out of my Saturday for that felt very aggressive to me, in a micro sort of way."

Christie laughs enthusiastically, leaning in slightly toward Logan before catching herself and inching away.

"Well, I just wanted to mention that it sounds like a few of us are going to get together tonight at Frog Horn for some drinks, if you don't have anything going on. And if my asking isn't too much of a microaggression, of course."

"That sounds great, actually, like really great," answers Logan. "But I've got a research meeting tonight in Bethesda. Maybe I can get away from the Old Man fairly early though. As long as I give him just enough time to tell me everything I'm doing wrong, he's usually satisfied. I'll shoot you a text when I finish."

* * *

The neighborhood is comprised primarily of multimillion-dollar homes, most of which seem strangely quiet and lacking in charm as the sun sets. Logan has arrived in front of a modest two-story home just after 7:00 p.m. The house is dated and out of place in this immaculate and wooded enclave of Bethesda, Maryland. He walks up the driveway, rings the doorbell, and waits momentarily as he observes through a window a petite elderly woman in her seventies with short white hair approaching the door inside. She opens the door and smiles warmly at Logan.

"Hello Maggie," says Logan, politely.

"He had his dialysis earlier today. I can't promise you he'll be in the best of moods. You want a cup of coffee? You might need it."

Suddenly a dog begins to bark, the annoying yap of a Scottish terrier. Logan enters the home while Lauren, the Old Man's assistant, emerges to drag away the yapping beast. Lauren is short, in her early twenties, with dark brown hair, pale skin, and impeccably chosen reading glasses. She is notorious for wearing bright colors and abnormally low-cut tops, all of which tend to provide a stark contrast against the dated, pastel-colored interior of the seventies-styled home. On the list of unpleasantries that accompanies a visit to his mentor, Lauren is fairly high, along with that dammed dog. Logan has been bitten by both, more times than he would care to acknowledge.

In the midst of the barking, ambiguous glares from Lauren, and Maggie bringing the coffee, a shout can be heard from the Old Man, coming from inside his basement office.

"Come on down," he shouts. "Grab some coffee if you want!"

Logan is eager to escape the chaos of the moment, although he remains reasonably trepidatious to get started with the patriarch of all this madness.

The Old Man is short and pudgy. There is a frailty in his movements. While others might have found him gentle and affable, with his bright white hair and elderly demeanor, he is stern with Logan. At best, his affect is perpetually neutral during their discourse, which is often less than reassuring for a young man with blue-collar origins trying to navigate the pompousness of elite academia. He had been a practicing psychiatrist for several decades prior to his pretend retirement, upon which, by all appearances, he still functioned as a practicing psychiatrist. He somehow still manages to teach a course on forensic profiling, but his voice has become so feeble at the podium that the complaints from students over inaudible lectures are becoming too prevalent to ignore. Logan covers for him when he can, although he is finding the Old Man's resistance to embracing his twilight years increasingly difficult to comprehend.

The Old Man is a relic leftover from a time when the intelligence community still valued a certain kind of intellect. The CIA had long been his true home, and the numerous ceremonial plaques and coins displayed in his office are a testament to his multitude of years spent helping US presidential administrations understand the minds of current foreign dictators, while working from within the halls of Langley to prevent the rise of new ones.

The office is dimly lit and maintains a setup conducive for sessions with psychiatry patients, with a couch and cushioned chairs that belie a once-expensive taste. In addition to his accolades for government achievement, the wood-paneled walls in the office are lined with various porcelain and tribal masks that provide for an eerie, yet mildly pretentious, environment. His desk is chaotic, with random journal articles and books strewn about, most of which were authored by the Old Man himself.

As Logan enters this Freudian proving ground, the Old Man greets him with a smile before quickly launching into his version of constructive criticism.

"I must say, I was quite disappointed with the draft you sent me. I was expecting you to have written more than that. I suspect we're going to get criticized for using such a crude factor analysis…"

Logan attempts to get a word in. A true exercise in futility. "Well, I agree, but I think we—"

The Old Man cuts him off quickly.

"—When we're profiling these lone wolf terrorists, we need to be more deliberate with our language, careful to note this is narcissistic grandiosity that is present, rather than delusional fantasies, which you occasionally refer to."

Logan listens with intent, suppressing any overt displays of frustration and shame. He tries to avoid the trap of a petulant child, as there is far more to this mentorship than a desperation to prove intellectual ambition.

"I completely agree," answers Logan. "Narcissistic grandiosity certainly seems more fitting. I'm wondering though if maybe you didn't see all of the changes I sent you in the—"

The Old Man interrupts, moving on to a new topic he is prone to introducing during these meetings with Logan. "I spoke to Tim on Monday," shares the Old Man. "It doesn't sound like there will be much in terms of part-time work while you're in school, but you should go ahead and submit your application for the Agency now…"

Logan again finds himself fighting to get a word in. "Really? You don't think it's too soon for..."

The Old Man goes on, oblivious to Logan's interjection. "And your Top Secret clearance, that expires when? It would be better if you could find a way to not let that expire. And you said your Russian is still pretty fluent?"

Logan's mind wanders off as the Old Man speaks. Logan is tired, and the dim lighting in this dated office does little to hide the dark circles around his eyes. He became acquainted with the Old Man shortly after beginning his graduate school journey, although there was nothing serendipitous about their encounter. The universities of the Washington, DC, metro area have long been prime recruiting grounds for various intelligence agencies, the sort of DC lore that many acknowledge with a wink and nod while self-righteously warning about loose lips without an air of irony. Thus, the relationship between these two men was just as much owed to destiny as it was to pragmatism.

* * *

Meetings with the Old Man can leave Logan with a strong urge to drink. He often finds himself practically holding his breath beforehand and desperately seeking a sigh of relief in the aftermath. Christie is somewhat of a welcome sight for him when he finds himself inside of a crowded DC bar surrounded by classmates later that evening. Logan has never been overly fond of crowded establishments, particularly in this town, where the ambient noise is so often tinged with status, optics, and neuroticism. But after a few drinks and some flirting with Christie, the environment becomes less of a concern.

Christie is leaning in close to him now, laughing uncontrollably as Logan does an impression of one of their professors. Occasionally her hand finds its way to his chest, this occurring in greater frequency as the beer flows. Logan can be quite charming, and he appreciates that Christie can be charmed.

"...and then he just stands there, with that bizarre smile on his face and weird lazy eye," jokes Logan. "How in the hell is this guy supposed to be a clinic director? If he was my therapist, I'd have to spend every session trying to look away from him. I wouldn't know whether he's trying to help me with my problems or lure me into his van with candy."

"Exactly! I'm glad you said it because I was starting to think I'm the only one who sees it," answers Christie enthusiastically.

A few classmates emerge to disrupt the romance and attempt to remind both that the next bar awaits. Logan, for a rare but brief moment, had just been starting to feel oblivious to the crowd around him. Christie is eager to persuade him to continue the night with their peers, although all of their classmates are aware that Logan has a penchant for disappearing into the night as a solo act. He is quite often a profound mystery to them, a trait which Christie can find alluring but others consider mildly off-putting. He has little desire to be in the midst of the party, or to be in the midst of anything at all.

"You're coming, right?" pleads Christie.

"I think I'm heading home actually. Been a long week. Too long."

Christie tries to conceal her disappointment. "Alright, your call. I'll see you on Monday."

Miles, a fellow graduate student less adept at handling his alcohol, interjects. "Logan! Come on man! I thought you were gonna show us those sweet dance moves tonight. I'll buy you a shot if you come with us!"

The group laughs, Logan included, before he politely declines. They all make their way for the exit before parting ways in separate directions. Logan continues to hear the faint sound of the group's laughter as the distance grows. There is some solace for him on a darkened city sidewalk. The Washington Monument looms in the background. He prefers DC when it's quiet.

* * *

Sitting at a small outdoor table on the rooftop of his apartment complex, Logan embraces the solitude later that night. Alone, with a half-empty bottle of bourbon and a lowball glass filled with whiskey and ice in front of him, his gaze is transfixed on a moment in the past. He stares straight ahead with cold, emotionless eyes as the sounds of sirens and the trickling of traffic continue through the night. If one were to stumble upon Logan in this moment, they would undoubtedly see a man in a dissociated state of sadness. And indeed, these flashbacks are nothing short of morose. This is the moment he has been reliving every night:

The aircrew in his ear, shouting.

"C.O. we gotta make a call. We're gonna lose him! We're gonna lose him! We're gonna lose him!"

Logan responding, "I'm calling it. I'm calling it. Standby for strike. I'm calling it."

And then, as always, the mutilated body of the Afghan male writhing around in the dirt, grasping for life.

It was that image, of the twisted, mangled body. There was something surreal and unshakeable about seeing a human body contorted in an unhuman manner. And there was a moral deprivation that haunted him.

He had played a role in the elimination of dozens of high-value targets, but on this mission he also had to witness the family finding what was left of their husband and father. This was the cost of taking a human life, even if it was a life that needed to be taken.

He never doubted that the men he hunted were bad men. He felt close to his targets though. They weren't friends or distant relatives. Logan was not an anthropologist but something more akin to a voyeur in hell. The enemy is easier to dehumanize when they're faceless and nameless. But the leadership, the bomb makers, the smugglers, sometimes they could be more ostentatious than the average opium farmer. They were emboldened, grandiose even. They thought they could travel unobstructed on a motorbike because their landscape wasn't meant for Westerners. Logan would meet them at that exact point that fate was tempted one too many times. But prior to the end, he always felt like he knew them after a multitude of intelligence briefings and weeks, sometimes months, of watching them and waiting. He did not have the luxury, or perhaps the mental constitution, of firing a weapon and then moving on. He kept their souls somewhere in a pocket next to his house keys and a flashlight.

War means asking mortal men to play God and somehow expecting them to shoulder the burden. When post-traumatic stress disorder arises in relation to war, it is simply the result of exposure to something that human beings are not meant to be exposed to. And so, on nights alone when he has a breather, he gasps. He had been to a therapist at the VA who tried to convince him that through a series of eye movements and tapping, he might no longer see the faces of the dead. He gave it three sessions. A different doctor in a different wing prescribed him an SSRI. It took him days to ejaculate, which made him wonder if the cure was perhaps worse than the disease. He stuck with it for just under two months. Ambien was given out like candy though. He would take it and stay awake for a while. It made the demons tangible but tolerable. He drank. He always had. Alcohol was part of the culture. But now he was finding himself increasingly spending more time drinking alone. This was new. It was as if he was pinned down by a paradox of wishing not to remember and choosing never to forget. He had returned from war an angrier man than he cared to admit. All he really wanted to do, consciously anyway, was drink, fuck, and fight. He had a fair amount of success with two of the three. A good woman was hard to keep around. Not because there were too few of them, but because he never thought of himself as being a good man. And he was too stubborn to be anyone's project.

Logan emerges from his flashback, eyes shifting back to his lowball glass. He looks exhausted. Emotion emerges, slightly. Tears form. The whiskey soothes. Eventually he falls asleep in his own bed that night, but never for long enough.

The next night, standing in front of a faded cream-colored door in the hallway of an old apartment building, the exhaustion has followed him. He can hear loud talking and laughter on the other side as he pauses before knocking, anticipating the joyful chaos of a reunion with old friends. The door swings open. John, his military friend, greets him warmly with a smile and a beer.

"Should we hug it out?" asks Logan.

John is inebriated. John is often inebriated. The two men share this in common.

After a quick hug and a pat on the back, Logan moves inside the apartment and is greeted by Alex, a second military friend, equally as drunk but twice as loud. Alex is Hispanic with a slight accent, chubby, with thick arms, a big untrimmed beard, and glasses. He tends to be excessively jovial, to the point no one can take him seriously, and thus no one does.

Riffing was a rite of passage for these men, and John can't help but point out how absurd Alex's beard looks.

"Check out Alex, rocking the homeless beard. Fairly certain there's a bird living in it!"

Logan chimes in, "Dude you look like the love child of Cat Stevens and the Unabomber!"

"Moonshadow!" shouts John.

Alex responds, "It is I! Cat Stevens Kaczynski!"

All three men laugh, each of them silently aware that they needed this comfort of being among their own dysfunctional brotherhood. In the background a DVD of a James Bond film plays on the TV. Logan knows the choice for entertainment is deliberate.

Once upon a time, on a boardwalk in Kandahar, Logan and John had stumbled into a makeshift storefront selling bootlegged American DVDs. The quality was usually so poor that they tended to be a film of a film, generally consisting of someone in Eastern Europe taking a camcorder into a movie theater. When this pirate would cough, the camera would shake. God forbid you buy a five-dollar DVD shot by a man during allergy season in Tbilisi. But when Logan and John rummaged through those DVDs one day, they both collectively discovered bootlegged James Bond boxed sets. This felt like Christmas morning in the middle of a warzone for both of them, and in that brief moment, the magic of Her Majesty's bootlegged lothario turned those men into boys. So when Logan shows up to John's apartment to find Mr. Bond in the background, this is John's subtle method of signaling that these men need each other, although they would hardly dare to admit it.

John hands Logan a beer as he settles onto a couch. They clink bottles.

"Cheers, man. For queen and country," answers Logan.

An inebriated Alex sits nearby, prompting a conversation from the newly arrived Logan.

"So when did you get out, man? They give you a hard time about not reenlisting?" Logan asks.

"Like two months ago," responds Alex, with that perpetual grin that always suggests a joke is on the way. "They were trying to entice me with all sorts of offers. Said they'd give me 60k up front."

"No shit?" responds a surprised Logan. "60k at once? Damn. Hell, I'll go learn some Arabic, maybe squeeze into a flight suit again for that kind of money."

"Dude, they're offering it for nearly everybody, Russian speakers too. They told me I could go back to being an Arabic linguist and no more of the ISR shit. Said I could have my choice to go anywhere I wanted. No more Kandahar. They're desperate."

"But they couldn't pull you back in, huh? School was calling? I don't blame you, man. I know you always dreamed of pursuing your studies in women's nineteenth-century feminist literature," jokes Logan.

"I was like fuuuuccckk that! I'm a college man now!" responds Alex, mimicking a silly walk with an air of superiority. "Gonna finish my bachelors and then hopefully get into a grad school somewhere. What about you? How's school going? Dude, I can't believe you're gonna be a doctor. Dr. Callahan!"

"It's going alright man. So fucking sick of sitting in a desk already though, listening to these rich kids complain about how stressed out they are. But nothing too challenging. You working anywhere?"

"Welllll, sort of," answers Alex. "I mean, I'm doing stuff, if you know what I mean." Alex once again has a sly, drunken smile on his face. He is purposely evasive, but far too drunk to keep up the act for long.

Logan answers in jest, "No, Cat Stevens, I have no idea what you mean, actually."

John, sitting nearby, shouts, "Moonshadow!"

More laughter permeates through the walls of John's small apartment.

"Welllll, I'm not really supposed to talk about it," answers Alex, clearly intending to talk about it nonetheless. "We should turn our phones off if we're going to chat about it."

All three men turn their phones off. The sudden seriousness feels like a nuisance to both Logan and John. They attempt to maintain some semblance of levity.

"So what's up?" asks Logan. "You some Columbian drug lord now?"

"So you guys remember how my dad works for ICE? Well he's got some connections with the FBI and mentioned to them that I was getting out but that I still speak some Arabic. Well apparently that sounded pretty appealing to the FBI, so they got ahold of me and asked me if I wanted to do some stuff for them."

John asks, "What kind of stuff? Like entertain at bar mitzvahs?"

The three friends laugh once again. Between the alcohol and a healthy dose of emotional avoidance, this is the kind of conversation all three would prefer to keep short.

Alex continues, "I wish! No, like, going to places, talking to people. I'm basically just like gathering intel for them."

"Well dude, that sounds a lot more interesting than spending every day learning how to test kids for ADHD or diagnosing depression," responds Logan.

"Yeah, well, I was thinking, they mayyy be looking for other people to help out too, if you ever want me to ask."

Logan answers, "Fuck it dude, might as well. Yeah, you can let them know I'm pulling my hair out sitting at a desk all day and I'm always down to take on some more intel work. My Russian is still pretty good, too."

Upon returning from war, your baggage consists of more than just bootleg DVDs. There are little demons that attach to the grooves of your mind. They are insidious, toying with your memories, your fears, keeping you alert, keeping you vigilant. And they are always eager to destroy a good night with the right recipe of alcohol, war stories, and moral injury.

Sometimes, impulse and stimulation-seeking become the primary methods for evading the painful. Avoidance of the past can interfere with the ability to apply scrutiny where scrutiny is needed. For Logan, an undying willingness to serve tends to keep his ambitions honorable. But it is also the sort of blind spot that is capable of becoming a man's undoing, honorable or not.

CHAPTER 3

The phone rings. Logan lies in bed, shirtless. The single nightstand next to his bed is lined with empty beer bottles and his now-ringing cell phone. The room is otherwise dark and bare, with little furniture and faint sunlight leaking in through the curtain window.

He had lived in hotels for years in the military, shifting around the country from one location to the next on the government's dime. He appreciated the thoroughness of the cleaning staff in Northern California. The remoulade on the burgers at the hotel restaurant in Mississippi. The proximity to honky-tonk saloons full of blondes in sundresses in Texas. Through all of this, he never unpacked his bags. There was no decorating, no reason to place his clothes in a dresser or pretend he was moving in. He had an acute awareness that all roads eventually would lead to war.

And now that he had seen such war up close, he remained confident in the inevitability of man's decline. Thus, he is still reluctant to unpack, to make a space his own. His phone stops ringing and the ding alerts him to a voice message. He presses play and hears the voice of Alex:

"Hey buddy. So those guys I told you about, the ones I'm kinda helping out, if you catch my drift, well they want to meet you. I'm gonna count on meeting you at your place at five, and then we can walk to the location. Alright, buddy, hopefully that works for you. See you in a couple hours."

Logan lets out an audible sigh and begins rubbing his eyes before he slowly crawls out of bed. He is already anticipating the beginning of something foolish. The truth is that he never takes Alex all that seriously, and he takes his own government even less so. But he is understimulated and willing to suspend his anticipatory suspicion for the sake of something, anything, that might make him feel alive again.

The Washington, DC, streets are busy on this particular Saturday evening. It is slightly overcast, and there is a chill in the air. Both men wear light jackets as they walk down the sidewalk. Given the circumstances, the weather feels appropriate for the mild paranoia both are hesitant to acknowledge. Alex begins to prepare Logan for a conversation that he is supposed to pretend he is not showing up to have.

"Well here's the thing, man. They can't know that I told you about any of this. As far as they know, I suggested to you that we should grab a drink at this cool whiskey bar I heard about, and so we're just a couple of dudes having a drink on a Saturday. And as far as you know, it's just gonna be you and I, nothing unusual—"

Logan interjects, "So I'm supposed to act like I don't see two random FBI-looking dudes staring at us and I should act surprised when they come up and start initiating conversation?"

"Well they'll probably, or maybe just my guy, will act like he spotted me at the bar and wanted to come say hello, as if he and I know each other somehow. There should be another guy with him, but I don't know how they'll do it. I don't know."

"You know, it would be a lot easier if we just skipped all this bullshit acting and approached them right from the get-go," responds Logan. "But I get it, man. Don't want them to think they can't trust you."

The sun is starting to set as the men open the door to a large rectangular-shaped whiskey bar. Logan had perhaps anticipated a dimly lit dive with a corner booth, but there is nothing remotely clandestine about this particular establishment. Bright lights and the DC set, with Patagonia vests and a wave of ostentatious chatter about K Street, J Street, and who is clerking for whom. Logan and Alex notice two seats at the bar open up serendipitously upon their entrance and hurry to claim them. An approaching bartender engages quickly.

"Hey guys, welcome. What can I get you?"

"Uh, just a Maker's, rocks, for me," responds Logan.

"You want a double?"

"That would be great, thank you."

"And what can I get you?" asks the bartender of Alex.

Alex hesitates. His nervous grin suggests a palette unaccustomed to so many options for bourbon.

"I'm not really a bourbon guy, or whiskey in general. But I feel like I gotta get something with whiskey because we're in a whiskey bar—"

"Sound logic, my friend," mutters Logan in jest.

"I could make you an old-fashioned. That's always a good option here."

"Yeah let's do that. That's kinda sweet, right? But not too sweet?"

"You got it," the bartender answers as he quickly shuffles away.

As they wait for their drinks, both men struggle to avoid taking in their surroundings. Without either of them knowing the location of the two FBI agents within the bar, there is a real fear that they might inadvertently make eye contact with them, spoiling the entire preposterous affair in the process. Ironically however, their efforts to maintain a low profile while seated at the bar have the unintended effect of making both Logan and Alex appear rather awkward as they stare straight ahead and speak in muffled tones. Theirs is a spycraft better suited for the tactical than the strategic, and a moment like this certainly blurs the lines between those modalities. Eventually, Logan would develop a mastery in both, but Alex was far too aloof to ever learn how to properly flip that switch.

The bartender brings the drinks, providing some liquid relief for the tension. It can be challenging to look natural when you're not sure where to place your hands, where to focus your gaze, and how loud your voice might carry.

"So how's this work? Are we just supposed to hang out for a while and hope your pal mysteriously bumps into you?" asks Logan.

Alex replies lightheartedly, "No clue, man. But damn this is a tasty beverage."

An hour passes. Logan is getting impatient. Suddenly, a voice excitedly calls out to Alex. Attached to the voice is a tall gentleman with blond hair, angular features, and a fresh shave. He has an all-American look to him, almost too clean-cut, as if he plays lacrosse in his off-hours and dreams of the glory days spent in a fraternity. The juxtaposition is apparent immediately. This man, thinks Logan, lacks the nonverbal intensity of the weathered military veteran.

"Alex?! Hey man! I thought that was you," calls out the all-American.

"Oh, Josh! What's up, man? What are you up to?" responds Alex. "Good to see you! This is my buddy Logan."

Josh extends his hand to Logan.

"Hey, I'm Logan. Nice to meet you. So how do you guys know each other?"

"I used to work with Alex's father a bit, so Alex and I would see each other on occasion."

"Oh with uh, ICE, right? Immigration and—"

"Well, actually I'm with the FBI. I do counterterrorism work, but yeah, I work with those ICE guys on occasion."

Logan was not expecting him to so readily confess as to his employer. Josh seems a little too eager to be affable, a little too desperate to appear forthcoming.

"Oh, awesome. Counterterrorism, huh? You want to pull up a seat, man, join us here at the bar?"

Josh responds, "Actually, yeah, I'd love to. Let me go grab my buddy, though. We were sitting down there at the other end. You guys mind if he joins us too? I'm not interrupting anything, am I?"

"Not at all, man," answers Alex. "The more the merrier."

Logan and Alex watch as Josh walks to the other end of the bar and approaches a table in the corner. In contrast to the boyish appearance of Josh, the man seated at this table has a muscular, slightly stocky frame, with a trimmed beard and short brown hair. He is of average height, wearing jeans with a long-sleeve shirt with the sleeves rolled up. A large black watch is attached to one wrist. Even from a distance, Logan recognizes a sort of palpable intensity to this man. He is not exactly low profile, but his absence of apparent charm suggests that few would feel compelled to glance for long in his direction. He strikes Logan as former military, or at least as a man desiring to appear as a combat veteran.

Josh exchanges a few unintelligible words with the bearded man. They both look over at Alex and Logan, exchange a few more words, and finally this second gentleman stands and joins Josh as they make their way over to Logan and Alex.

Josh makes the introduction. "Hey guys. This is my buddy Brock. Brock, this is Alex and, uh, Logan, right?"

"Yeah, Logan. Nice to meet you, man."

Logan extends his hand and is met with a firm handshake. Brock's nonverbals are no less intense up close, as he includes piercing eye contact and a head nod with the grip.

"So, what are you guys drinking there?" inquires Brock.

Logan responds, "Well I've got a little Maker's on the rocks here, and I believe Alex has—"

A nervous Alex interjects. "I went with an old-fashioned. I'm not really much of a whiskey guy but it seemed like a good choice."

In the midst of this very brief moment, Logan recognizes a shift in Alex's demeanor. Something about Brock has left Alex feeling noticeably uneasy. This is perhaps not the first time these men have interacted, a thought that Logan chooses to keep to himself.

"Very nice. So what are you fellas up to?" asks Brock.

Logan responds casually. "Oh just out having a drink or three. I was actually about to pick Josh's brain a bit. He was just telling us that he works in counterterrorism. Are you in a similar line of work?"

"Uh, yeah, I work for the Bureau too, but I'm in counter-intel. What about you guys?"

The tone of Brock's voice seems incongruent with his posture. He might be former military, but he speaks with the cadence of a man accustomed to defusing tension. Perhaps he was adept at conversing with tribal elders in Afghanistan as a soldier. Or, perhaps he was a public affairs officer once attached to a Special Forces unit. Perhaps the oversized watch and the working-class attire are simply the tells of a man whose real skillset lies in fashioning a narrative. Logan's skepticism points him toward the latter. But these mental calculations could cost him an advantage in interpersonal dynamics, so he snaps out of it quickly.

"Well, I'm going to school right now, at GW. I'm working on my doctorate in clinical psychology—"

Brock interrupts with a comment stroking Logan's ego, a pattern Logan will soon come to recognize.

"So what you're saying is that you're a genius then?" jokes Brock.

Logan laughs briefly. "I wouldn't go that far. I will say I do some research on the side, though, that I'm quite proud of, on lone wolf terrorism, basically developing psychological profiles on lone wolf terrorists, examining that radicalization process."

"Oh wow, very nice. Big need for that! Awesome, man," responds Brock, enthusiastically.

Logan adds, "That's actually why I'm pursuing my doctorate, so I can make a career out of psychological profiling in the intelligence community. I used to work in intel in the military too."

Brock and Logan continue their conversation for quite some time. Logan talks more than is necessary, but he can't help but feel like he is in a job interview for a job he's supposed to pretend doesn't exist.

An hour passes before the two FBI agents finally prepare to say goodbye.

"Tell your father I said hello," remarks Josh to Alex, as he noticeably pats Alex on the shoulder, an earnest gesture that conveys approval of a job well done. He moves to shake Logan's hand next.

"Logan, it was nice meeting you. Keep it up with that research, man. Definitely sounds like something that would be very helpful to us some day—"

"Yeah actually, I'd be interested in reading some of your work and maybe pick your brain a bit more about it," interjects Brock. "Would love to shoot you an email sometime soon to continue the conversation."

"Absolutely man. I look forward to hearing from you. Take care guys."

And with that, a bewildering evening reached its conclusion.

* * *

Two weeks would pass before Logan receives the slightest indication as to whether he made a positive impression. Two long weeks spent desperately hoping for a disruption to the monotony of graduate school life. He was told he was privileged to have a seat in such esteemed classrooms, but this has begun to feel like a transition from killing terrorists to the slow death of his own vitality. But then one quiet afternoon, as he is sitting at a small wooden table near the bookshelves that help to comprise his very limited array of furniture in his otherwise bare apartment, a quick ding from his open laptop alerts him to an email. Finally, word from the boys at the Bureau. Brock's email reads:

> Hey man, it was great meeting you guys the other night at the bar. Your work combining psychology and intel is fascinating stuff. We should get together and talk more about it. I think it might be applicable to some of the work I'm involved in. Are you available tomorrow night? If so, let's grab drinks at Otis Tavern, 5 p.m.? Let me know.—Brock

CHAPTER 4

Otis Tavern. Washington, DC. 5:00 p.m. EST.

The dimly lit tavern is mostly empty as the two men occupy a booth in the corner. The establishment is stylish, with mahogany tints, rustic lightbulbs hanging from the ceiling, and soul music playing softly. The venue selection feels a little too deliberate to Logan, as if the tone is taking precedent over the practicality. The first cocktail eases the tension. With the second, Brock's pitch begins.

"So, that ability to talk to people like that, to get them to open up and talk about their problems, that's definitely a skill that's hard to come by. My only question is, can you do it in Russian?" asks Brock.

"Russian?" a curious Logan replies.

"Yeah. I've read your files. Top of your class in intel school. Graduated with a three three in Russian. That's unheard of. Hell, I've even seen your SERE footage. It's impressive. So you go through all that training, but then they send you off on 137 combat missions in Iraq and Afghanistan. And the whole time your Russian abilities are just lying there, dormant, unused, wasted. So I ask again, can you do it in Russian? Could you sit down next to somebody and strike up a conversation, casually, in Russian, and get them to like you, to tell you about themselves? Could you tell them about yourself in Russian?"

This was far from the discussion Logan had been anticipating. The initial feigned interest in his research now felt like a bait and switch. This was not about counterterrorism. This was about counterintelligence.

"We're not here to talk about my research, are we?" asks Logan.

"No. Remember when I said I work in counterintel? My specific target is Russia. As I'm sure you're aware, there's been a helluva increase in Russian espionage activities over the last few years, including right here in our nation's capital. Ever since Snowden, the Russians have been recruiting heavily, trying to find the next Snowden, the next American with a bright future in the intelligence community, who they can bring over to their side. There's actually a restaurant, or club really, here in DC, where we know they're operating out of. I'd like you to start frequenting this place, gathering intel for us. And we don't need to know everything at once. It's all about the long game. Introduce yourself, talk to people, see who pokes their head out."

"So you want to use me as bait, as a dangle, to see who comes out of the weeds, who takes an interest in somebody like me?"

Brock, sensing some remaining incredulity, begins to sweeten the pot.

"Listen, if you do this, it could be huge for US government interests. There could be some money in it for you; we could help you land a job in the intelligence community later down the road. And, I should mention this, if you're working with us, just consider that you can do anything necessary to further the mission. You don't have to worry about what's legal, what's not legal. You'd be working for us. I know you want to get back to catching bad guys. Let us help you with that."

Logan is reluctant to appear too eager, too curious. He had been programmed as a machine, conditioned to suppress emotion, to demonstrate mathematical precision for the sole purpose of a singular objective: Study a target. Eliminate the target. Receive a new target.

The classroom is easy for him, but entirely foreign at this stage of his life. There is no risk, no postmission existential dilemma about living and dying. He is bored, and boredom is dangerous for him. Brock intends to exploit that. Logan is sure of it. But he cannot run. Some distant algorithm brought him here, ensuring his answer would be yes. He keeps up with the theatrics nonetheless. There is an element of play in all of it. Roles on top of roles. He thinks of Shakespeare: "And one man in his time plays many parts."

And then he snaps back to the present moment. Maintain doubt. Be incredulous. Let the agent play his role.

"So let me get this straight," responds Logan. "You guys have millions of dollars in your budget, the freedom to monitor anybody you want thanks to FISA, and the full force of the United States government behind you, and you're telling me you need some grad student to mingle with Russian foreign agents over drinks?"

"Precisely. Look, there's the way business is normally done, yeah, but we wanna try something new with you. Normally, as I'm sure you're aware, there's this very tit-for-tat game we play with them, where we go after their guys, and then they return the favor by hitting us in Moscow or somewhere else.

"Let's say, hypothetically, you've got some fancy hotel here in DC where we know some of their embassy guys like to get their rocks off. So our guys burst in, catch some shocked, chubby, balding sixty-five-year-old in bed with a masculine-looking prostitute in cheap lingerie, male anatomy barely hidden. Let's just say she's packing some heat. This kinda thing would be embarrassing for baldy if word got back to Moscow. So now we got him. But, so the story goes, we catch them in a honeypot, and next thing you know they're killing the dogs of our diplomats in Latvia. Literally. Some jacked Russian dude in, let's say, hypothetically again, a beige trench coat and black leather gloves, stands in the middle of an apartment while the American tenants are out, and point-blank executes a golden retriever with a PSS silent pistol. Why? Because two hours later an American couple, husband is your standard diplomat with thick glasses and a smug look, and wife is somehow a gorgeous blonde in a fur coat, they walk into their apartment full of laughs and feeling like life is rainbows and butterflies, only to shriek in terror when they find the blood of their precious Stella splattered across their clean white living room. Message sent, message received, right?

"Or here's a good one for you. You take the suburbs around here, let's say NOVA. Let's say you got a guy working for our government. The sort of guy who has a TS clearance and knows things. Let's say this guy has a habit of going for walks on trails through a wooded park near his neighborhood. Let's say once every couple of months, this gentleman likes to duck under a small wooden bridge on one of these aforementioned trails and place an envelope on a ledge, an envelope which is always picked up two hours later by some Russian illegals posing as Johnny and Susie down the block. Well, one day the gig is up and SWAT team ensures all parties involved have a very bad day. No more dead drop, only embarrassment. And how do they retaliate? Well, they beat the shit out of our guys in Moscow. I could tell you the tale of a certain American official desperately trying to reach our embassy in Moscow in the middle of the night, only to have a Russian guard stationed in a booth immediately outside of the compound tackle the dude and beat the shit out of him just as he starts to take out his badge. The Russians will chalk it up to 'mistaken identity.' Meanwhile, our guy is hospitalized with fractured ribs, busted eye socket, broken nose, broken collar bone, and so on. Taken out of the game. 'Mistaken identity.'

"Now, let's say, hypothetically, we shut down one of their diplomatic buildings here in DC after we very publicly link it to an espionage ring. I mean, news flash, they're all fucking linked to an 'espionage ring,' but we take action when we need to send a message. They'll scramble, try to burn everything. You'll see something on the news about punitive measures, blah blah blah. And how do they retaliate? Ever heard of acoustic attacks? Imagine you're a US diplomat stationed in Cuba, sitting in your apartment reading a newspaper, trying to have a nice quiet morning, and suddenly this really high-pitched, steady tone can be heard throughout your house, like the chirping of a cricket that never ends. Dude falls off the couch onto his knees, places his fingers from both hands onto the temples on both sides of his head and closes his eyes tightly. He's in excruciating pain, moaning in agony, before keeling over and vomiting onto his floor. He'll never be the same after that."

Logan listens with intent, silently wondering how long Brock had rehearsed this speech, and how many times had he uttered these same words previously. Surely Logan was not the first man of such restrained social stature to be asked to embark on such a preposterously ambitious endeavor. Regardless, the long, anecdotal pitch is largely unnecessary. Logan has little reason to trust Brock or any of this, but his answer is going to be yes just the same. For as analytical and methodical as he can be, boredom can either light a man's fire or smother it, and Logan has been in search of a spark.

* * *

Logan's mission begins only three nights later. The alluring nocturnal ambience of the bustling, posh DC neighborhood draws in the Eastern European club girls like bats in a neon city. This is no paradise for working-class men. Wealth and influence are currencies, and Logan has neither. He is capable of being mysterious though, making sure the only cards that are easy to read are the ones he wants you to see. This will have to do.

As Logan walks down the city sidewalk, he approaches a multistory restaurant with a sign that reads "Bolshoi Mir." He is dressed in business-casual attire, wearing a blazer and slacks. Although the intent with his sartorial choices was to blend in, he looks a bit more professorial than he would have liked. When he reaches the front of the restaurant, he glances at a small collapsible sign out front listing the dinner and drink specials for the night. Casually peering through the window, he observes a crowded restaurant with an inordinate amount of fur coats and short skirts. He takes a deep breath, pauses, and enters.

The interior of Bolshoi Mir resembles a large Russian mansion full of elaborate chandeliers, trinkets, and classic Russian decorations. Tables are scattered throughout, full of patrons eating Russian cuisine and drinking various alcoholic beverages. Vodka, potatoes, and perfume permeate the air. At the far end of the restaurant a stairwell is visible, leading up to a second and third floor. A very faint thumping sound of club music can be heard traveling down the stairwell and arriving directly into Logan's ears. On initial impression, he surmises his night will likely end up somewhere on those upper levels. In the meantime though, Logan quickly notices that the servers in the downstairs restaurant are all outrageously attractive Russian women. The entire setting feels somewhat peculiar, as if Logan has entered a country within a country, albeit one with an intense respect for minding the culture of a homeland. A respect likely enforced via the large muscular men scattered throughout the venue who appear to be providing security, all wearing dark-colored suits and earpieces. The level of security seems out of place, perhaps even excessive, in the quaint, old-world Russian atmosphere.

Logan, standing in the entrance, quickly eyes an empty seat at the bar, immediately to the right of the front door. Perhaps out of habit, he is inclined to choose the vantage point most conducive for threat assessment and egress. Not exactly a bold move, he thinks to himself, but this is no time to appear overly confident. As he moves to sit, there is a palpable sense of eyes upon him. He casually takes in the setting. The wall behind the bar is lined with endless bottles of vodka. Small TVs, on both ends, are playing black-and-white Soviet-era Russian cartoons. Directly attached to the wall in front of him is a mysterious wooden box, opened for all to see, displaying several rows of identical skeleton keys.

As he takes in his surroundings, while coming to terms with the absurdity of his assignment, he notices the gorgeous female bartender has shot a glance in his direction. She wears a short dark skirt and a top that somehow manages to be both revealing and conservative simultaneously. The bartender approaches.

"Hi. What would you like to drink?" She speaks with a slight, sexy, Russian accent.

"Hmm, I don't really know what I'm in the mood for. Any recommendations? This is my first time here."

"I can make you a Moscow mule."

Her short, direct statements, combined with a relative coldness toward Logan, makes him think that her demeanor is due less to a language barrier and more to an indifference toward newcomers. Besides, Logan might be out of his element, but his cultural expertise is fortunately advanced enough to know that Moscow mules are for American men who only think they're drinking an authentic Russian beverage. Logan plays along.

"Moscow mule? That's like ginger beer and vodka, right? As long as it has vodka, I suppose it counts as Russian, right? That sounds great. Thank you."

Her lips form a slight smile as she walks off to make Logan's drink. Somewhere among the cacophony of barroom noise, he overhears a patron refer to the bartender as "Sasha." Obtaining this singular name feels like a silly victory, but a victory nonetheless.

Logan sits alone at the bar, casually glancing at his phone as he covertly attempts to listen to the other conversations around him while he waits for his drink. The chatter is all meaningless small talk in English. Out of the corner of his eye, he catches a glimpse of another lonely drinker. Sitting at the opposite end of the bar, the man appears to be an American, of average height with reddish hair, likely in his early thirties. The man is scrolling through his phone just as Logan inadvertently makes a bit too much eye contact, drawing the man's attention. He looks up, smiles, and nods his head slightly. Logan reciprocates the gesture, which the lonely drinker apparently interprets as an invitation for dialogue. He stands from his seat, grabs his drink, and approaches Logan.

"This seat taken?" The accent is perfectly American, albeit mildly slurred. Logan immediately evaluates the pros and cons of befriending an inebriated American. The gamble pays off in short order.

"Please, feel free," responds Logan.

"I'm Kevin," slurs the new friend as he extends his hand.

"Hi, I'm Logan. Have you—" Sasha approaches with drink in hand, just as Logan attempts small talk. An excited Kevin flashes her a big smile and speaks to her briefly in Russian.

"Ah, Sasha! Krasivaya zhenshina! Ochen krasivaya zhenshina. Dy-tyu, pozhalsta, vodka, oh-pyat. (Beautiful woman, very beautiful woman! Please give me vodka again.)"

Sasha responds, "Konyeshna! (Of course!)"

She winks at Kevin and flashes a smile before walking away to get his vodka. Valuable data, Logan thinks. Valuable data.

Logan offers a compliment. "That sounded like some pretty excellent Russian."

"Spasiba! (Thank you!) You speak Russian?"

Logan answers effectively, although perhaps a bit rusty. "Ni minoga, ni minoga (not much). Just a little bit. I studied it in the military."

In an exaggerated gesture, Kevin points a finger at Logan and in an animated tone begins to speak in Russian.

"Ohn spion! Ohn spion! (He's a spy! He's a spy!)"

Logan and Kevin both share a laugh at the preposterous notion that a spy would show up to such an establishment and casually sit at the bar.

"I wish it was that exciting," answers Logan. "Truth is, I never even got to use the language. Ended up doing intelligence work in Iraq and Afghanistan instead. But, that's why I wanted to come here. I heard about this place and thought it might be a good opportunity to practice my language skills a bit."

As Logan speaks, an attractive Russian waitress in a short skirt walks past both of them. They turn and stare, making little effort to hide their gaze.

"Oh you can practice a lot of things around here!" proclaims Kevin.

Both men share a laugh.

"Well, I'm afraid my language abilities are lacking a bit compared to yours," adds Logan.

As the men converse, Sasha emerges with a vodka for Kevin. Logan seizes the opportunity to demonstrate just enough Russian language capability to feed into Kevin's curiosity.

"Ya bui ho-tel zakazat vodka tozha, pazhalsta. (I would like a vodka also, please.)"

An enthusiastic Kevin shouts in reply, "Ah, there you go! Not bad!"

"So what about you, how'd you learn to speak Russian so well?" inquires Logan.

"Oh, I took a couple of classes in undergrad at Columbia."

There are probably a dozen answers Kevin could have offered that would have made far more sense than the one he supplied, but Logan chooses not to push. Data for later, he thinks as he offers a curt reply.

"Oh, cool. Very nice."

Kevin, with an apparent eagerness to change the subject, asks, "Have you been upstairs yet? There's a whole other floor. That's where the best women are at."

Logan replies, "No, but what are we waiting for!?"

Rising from their barstools, the two men make their way toward a set of L-shaped stairs. With each step a faint sound of thumping club music grows louder in Logan's ears. Halfway up the stairs, on a landing, stands a muscular security guard in a suit, with an earpiece. He mutters something into the earpiece and nods at the men as they walk past. The walls of the stairwell are adorned with classical paintings by Russian artists. Elaborate, beautiful chandeliers hang from the ceiling. As they reach the top of the stairs, an open set of doors reveals a dimly lit club, with black leather couches against brick walls. The thumping begins to reach a disorienting crescendo for Logan. Between the tinnitus that has plagued him since his proximity to a mortar round was once closer than he cares to admit, and the surging adrenaline he is actively working to hide, he must remind himself to keep one foot in front of the other.

Walking through the entrance, they are met with the sight of beautiful, scantily dressed Russian women, joyfully moving and swaying on the dance floor. No less than half of them appear to be accompanied by much older, slightly chubby Russian men. Logan doubts it was their charisma and charm that earned them their dances. He suppresses the urge to laugh and continues following Kevin, who leads the way to the bar tucked in the corner. Kevin immediately addresses a tall, muscular Russian gentleman in the midst of pouring drinks behind the bar.

"Ah, Dmetri! Moi tovareesh! (My comrade!) This is my new friend Logan."

Dmetri is sporting a short-sleeve, skin-tight shirt, and Logan takes a mental note of the tattoo sleeves that adorn both of Dmetri's arms. Dmetri nods at Logan and then quickly responds to Kevin, in English, with a tone that feels relatively solemn in comparison to Kevin's boisterous energy.

"How are you, my friend?"

"We would love a couple of drinks, please," answers Kevin.

A mischievous grin overtakes Dmetri's face. "I have a new vodka, just for you. It's peppered, but a bit spicy. Can you handle that? On the house."

Logan's mind runs through a number of microsecond mental computations trying to assess the probability of whether he's about to drink something he will later regret. His primary question is whether he will wake up in his own bed that night or come to with a knife wound in an alley. Regardless, there is no turning back, not now. Dmetri pours three shots, one each for Logan and Kevin and one for himself. Shot glass raised, Logan takes the initiative.

"Za zdrovya! (Cheers!)" proclaims Logan with an ambitious fervor meant to mask his silent trepidation. He might speak the language, but his blood is Irish, and vodka rarely goes down smoothly. This seems to be an exception though. The spice carries a mild sting, but the overall taste from start to finish is impeccably delicious. A little too delicious. The variable of where he might wake remains unknown, but at least it will apparently be by his own volition.

Dmetri begins to pour the next round while Kevin's attention has meanwhile shifted to an attractive female server nearby. He calls out to her, demonstrating once again a familiarity with all the right faces.

"Katya! Come say hello!" shouts Kevin.

She approaches with a less than enthused look on her face. A pattern is emerging, thinks Logan. Perhaps to some in this establishment, Kevin is more notorious than he was a celebrated figure, but he is also tolerated. Why? Is he useful? A big spender? Or simply someone the staff can laugh at behind closed doors?

"Hello Kevin," utters a slightly deadpan Katya with an American accent. She is small in stature, with a slightly pointed nose and dark hair. Her skirt is short and her blouse revealing, all dark colors that punctuate her pale skin and smokey eye-shadow. There is a ferocity in her posture, perhaps born of an occupation spent responding to men like Kevin.

"Have you missed your favorite customer?" asks Kevin, as he moves in to give her an unwanted hug. Katya opts not to reciprocate the gesture, letting her arms just hang at her side until the experience has ended. "This is my new friend Logan. He's a spy!"

Katya cracks a slight smile and greets Logan with a hand-shake.

"Nice to meet you, Mr. Spy."

"It's a pleasure to meet you," responds Logan, suddenly becoming acutely aware of Katya's sultry magnetism.

Katya grabs a tray from the bar and walks away, carrying Logan's gaze along with every step. He returns to the present moment.

"You keep telling people I'm a spy and I bet they'll kick me out of here in no time!" remarks Logan with a sardonic grin.

Kevin replies with equal jest, "Oh trust me, my friend, you'll be safe with your pal Kevin. None of us are really who we say we are anyway, right? I get treated like royalty here. You can be too. I even have my own key. A special key."

The comment is cryptic. Bait for Logan, from a man who enjoys his notoriety while desperately wishing for an ounce of sincerity that few maintain toward him after an initial encounter.

Insufferable is the word that comes to mind, as Logan begins to grapple with the tediousness of Kevin's showmanship. He is hesitant to bite, but knows he must. Failure to inquire about the purpose of such a key might appear more peculiar than an expression of curiosity. When it comes to Russian intelligence services though, he knows that the sweeter the bait, the deadlier the trap.

"Moi tovareesh (My friend), you cannot tempt me with such a curiosity and at this point expect that I won't desperately be interested in obtaining such a key for myself! What riches, may I ask, does it unlock? A back room full of the finest caviar? Access to Dmetri's secret vodka stash?"

Kevin belts out a hearty laugh. He is a schoolboy relishing in the power of dangling a secret that will make him popular for a day. Logan has played to his ego. This is the game.

CHAPTER 5

A café in Alexandria. 12:05 p.m. EST.

The quiet café is mostly empty and resembles something buried in a time capsule twenty years prior. As Logan pulls into the parking lot, he cannot help but feel this location might be a poor choice if the two stern-looking gentlemen he spots seated inside near the window want to appear as anything other than federal officers. Brock has brought a partner, which seems like an escalation of sorts to Logan, although exactly how or why remains a mystery for now.

Brock and Harry watch from inside as Logan steps out of his truck and makes his way to the entrance. Harry appears older than Brock, clean-shaven with a square jaw.

"This our guy?" asks Harry.

"Yep, that's him," remarks a stone-faced Brock.

Logan swings open the door to the café and immediately makes eye contact with the two FBI agents, giving them a quick nod before approaching. He wonders if he should be more hesitant. He wonders how the two men might signal to him to avoid an approach if an unforeseen risk has emerged. He wonders if they wonder, if they give a second thought to the risks taken by men they recruit to do their bidding. His best guess, thus far, is that Brock won't lose sleep over spilled milk. A source is just a means to an end for them. Logan will try to remind himself of this, again and again. Such is the folly of service before self.

"Gentleman," declares Logan as he grabs his seat.

"Hey man, how's it going? This is my partner, Harry."

Harry and Logan shake hands, a gesture feels awkward due to the blank, sullen look that Harry maintains. The odd distrust is palpable, although no fault of Logan's.

"Did you eat? You want to order something? We're in no rush," remarks Brock. He adds, "It's on us, of course."

"I'm good for now, but thank you."

"Alright, well in that case, let's hear it. How'd the night go? You drink a shitload of vodka and then get crazy with some of those Russian chicks? Tell me about this guy Kevin. Something seemed off about him?"

Logan responds but chooses not to mirror Brock's enthusiasm. "Well, the dude says he's American, speaks with an American accent, and yet he speaks flawless Russian. Nothing too strange there, right? Except, he claims he learned Russian from taking a couple classes in undergrad at Columbia. Nobody picks up on Russian like that from a couple of undergrad classes."

"So you think he's lying?" asks an incredulous Harry.

"Something is going on, that's for sure. This dude spots me probably as soon as I walk in. I had barely been sitting at the bar when he approaches. He's super friendly. Immediately wants to start chatting. Who knows, maybe this is just a guy who likes to be social while he drinks. He was so forward with his approach, I actually wondered if maybe he was another one of your guys."

This last remark from Logan produces an opportunity to observe the intricacies of Brock and Harry's nonverbal communication. Brock, appearing convincingly curious, shoots Harry a quick glance. Without a word, Harry shakes his head no.

Logan continues. "So anyway, as Kevin starts chatting with me, it soon becomes clear that this dude seems to know everybody that works in the place. There's the bartender, Sasha, and her possible boyfriend, Dmetri, the upstairs bartender. Kevin tells me the two of them have been having some relationship issues. He didn't elaborate. There's also Katya, a server upstairs. Katya seems to despise Kevin. There's a history there, but again, he didn't elaborate. Anyway, Katya is smoking hot. American accent. No clue if she speaks Russian or what her story is. So anyway, the night unfolds with Kevin getting numerous free shots for us from Dmetri upstairs and Kevin of course hinting all night that he gets treated like royalty at Bolshoi Mir. And nothing I saw seemed to contradict that. At one point, he goes so far as to claim he has his own key, some kind of special key given to VIPs at the club. And I did, in fact, notice some kind of ornamental wooden box attached to the wall behind the bar downstairs, which was displayed open, revealing an interior that held dozens of identical skeleton keys. Presumably, these are the keys Kevin was talking about. The key thing struck me as peculiar at first, a novelty, but then…"

Brock interjects, "I do want to get back to the keys, but first, remind us about Kevin's story. Where he's from, what he does."

A mildly frustrated Logan raises no qualms about this disruption to his flow. Human intelligence operations (HUMINT) can be at once both critical and deeply flawed. Sources are often kept in the dark about the game that is being played, and this exploitation is a pill that Logan can swallow thus far. His solace is in playing a game of his own. How close can he stand to the flame before the burn sets in?

"Well, he was not very forthcoming with personal information," replies Logan. "Sounded like he went to Columbia for undergrad and then spent some time in Poland doing some work, although he once again did not elaborate. Now he is supposedly a fellow at the Hale Institute for Foreign Affairs in DC."

"The think tank?" responds a mildly intrigued Harry.

Logan wonders silently whether this is what enthusiasm looks like in Harry's world.

"Yep, that's the one," responds Logan.

There is a slight shift in energy at the table. Logan suspects he has shared something of value, but the moment passes quickly as Brock redirects the conversation.

"So, what about these keys?"

"Yes, the keys," responds Logan. "Wooden box, open for the world to see. It's not exactly something they're trying to hide. But you gentlemen tell me if perhaps my imagination was a bit too active initially, because when Kevin first starts hinting at this whole key thing, my mind immediately wanders to drugs or women."

"Why?" asks Harry, returning to his original sternness.

"Why not? The club, the chandeliers, servers wearing next to nothing, secret backrooms. I'm no expert on the Russian escort industry in this town, but as former military, I can confidently say that I know my way around strip clubs, from the high end to the trailer parks. Whatever this key situation was, I knew it wasn't twenty-dollar lap dances and recent C-section scars. But alas, I couldn't leave you boys wanting, so I took Kevin's bait and asked. He tells me that the keys are for VIPs. Says that on occasion the Bolshoi Mir will hold special events that only keyholders can attend. He was fairly cryptic, but alluded to a few prior events. Special-release vodkas. Women in lingerie. 'Real power players present,' his words. So now I'm thinking the club is very selective about who gets a key. People with influence."

"In this town," responds Harry, "the people with influence are usually the most at risk of being influenced."

"More money, more problems," adds Brock, with an attempt at levity.

Logan, sensing the conversation is nearing its conclusion, adds, "Well you guys are the secret agents here; you tell me. It didn't feel like a half bad first night."

"This is all great stuff, man," responds Brock. "You're a natural. I mean that. I was just telling Harry that I'm looking forward to seeing what all you can do. Sounds like you're already on the right track."

Logan tries his best not to acknowledge the compliments, but a subtle look of pride and self-reflection on a job well done flashes across his face. He feels vulnerable because he is. A man who seeks approval from a snake will still suffer the consequences of a bite just the same.

"Yeah, I think I've got some good groundwork there done that'll continue helping me meet some new faces. Speaking of which, Kevin suggested I swing by one night during the week to meet up with him for karaoke night at Bolshoi Mir. He said it's a little quiet inside during the week, but there's usually a small group that loves singing in Russian. Should be interesting. Would give me a chance to learn more about him."

"Sounds like you're headed to karaoke night, then," replies Brock. "Hopefully you've been warming up your singing voice. So when can you go back?"

* * *

A week later, on a late Washington afternoon, Logan emerges from an exterior side door to a drab classroom building on his campus. With a black backpack slung over his shoulder, he begins making his way down the sidewalk and away from the brutalist architecture that plagues those particular city blocks. His escape is short-lived, however, as the voice of his classmate Christie calls out to him.

"Hey, Logan! I've never seen you in such a mad rush to get out of class. Everything alright?"

Christie's normally soft-spoken and academic demeanor is eclipsed by a bright smile she flashes toward Logan.

He's almost annoyed. He's got places to be. "Hey, sorry, yeah. I've got this stupid research thing that I'm kinda stressing out about. It's my own fault for putting it off until now."

"Damn," replies Christie. "Was hoping we could still study for that psychopathology midterm tonight. Guess you won't be around?"

Logan pauses. She has a smile that he doesn't want to feel responsible for removing.

"Actually, um, yeah probably not until like 10 p.m., which I'm guessing is a little late for you."

Christie is not deterred.

"No, 10 p.m. works really well. That gives me time to finish some treatment notes. I'll see you at your place."

Before Logan turns to continue on his journey, Christie moves in and abruptly kisses him on the cheek. It's unexpected. She flashes him another smile and walks away in the opposite direction. Logan cycles through one round of a deep inhale and a deep exhale, feeling both perplexed and slightly amused at the brief interaction. He watches a bubbly Christie trot away and then continues his walk through the city.

CHAPTER 6

A lonely bar at Bolshoi Mir. 5:08 p.m. EST.

Logan finds himself sitting at a mostly empty bar. Although it's fairly early and on a weeknight, he had still anticipated something a bit more lively. Few patrons occupy the restaurant and very little foot traffic travels the stairs to the upper levels. Logan is turned slightly away from the bar to face Katya, the server with the American accent. An observer from afar might call this flirting. An observer from up close might damn well call it chemistry. Katya begins the conversation carrying a tray, but she reveals no hint to suggest that she is in much of a hurry to end the conversation. Logan, feeling bold, makes his move.

"Well, if you're interested," remarks Logan, "I'd love to get a drink sometime, maybe practice our Russian."

Katya's reply is sufficiently cheeky.

"I don't know if it's wise to get a drink with a spy. Besides, between school and work, I hardly have a free night. But I suppose I could find some time for a cup of coffee."

"Oh, coffee with a spy is a bit safer, huh?" responds Logan.

She blushes and laughs as she starts to walk away, tray in hand, offering a final comment to end with a smile.

"Mozhit beet, spion! (Maybe, spy!)"

As Katya walks away, Logan turns to face forward at the bar. The TV mounted on the wall silently plays the usual old Soviet cartoons that are starting to feel familiar to him. Logan watches for a brief few moments and then pulls out his cell phone, pretending to read the news on his phone as he casually listens to the few conversations occurring around him.

Dmetri, the tall, muscular Russian bartender Logan had met during his previous visit, is working behind the bar. He approaches.

"Logan, right? Welcome back, my friend. What can I get you? Vodka? I have a new one, it's peppered, but a bit spicy. What do you think?"

Logan stares up at Dmetri in an awkward moment of silence, finding the interaction peculiar, as Dmetri had uttered the same words only days earlier at the upstairs bar. How very odd, he thinks, how very odd.

"That sounds great," responds Logan with a smile.

Dmetri turns and grabs a bottle, pouring two shots. He places one in front of Logan and holds the other up.

"Cheers, my friend," states an eager Dmetri.

Logan raises his shot glass to meet the moment. Down it goes. An excited Dmetri immediately wants feedback.

"What do you think? It's good, yes? My own creation. Have you tried the honey vodka? It's nice to have something sweet after the spice. Let me get you one."

Before Logan has a chance to respond, Dmetri turns and grabs another bottle. He fills the same two shot glasses. Without hesitation, matched in balletic synchronicity, the shots go down. The vodka burns as Logan swallows. He tries his best to pretend otherwise, but Dmetri is particularly attuned to these sorts of reactions.

"Ah, don't like this one, huh? Hmm, let me think, what about—"

Logan laughs and cuts him off. "I think I'll need a minute, Dmetri. Maybe a beer would help?"

"No problem, my friend. Peevo ee vodka! (Beer and vodka!)"

Logan laughs again as Dmetri fills a beer and another shot for him.

"I suppose I am here to drink like a Russian after all."

"In that case, you have a lot of work to do, my friend," jokes Dmetri.

Logan responds, "Well hopefully Kevin can help me out. Have you seen him? He's supposed to meet me here tonight for karaoke."

A confused look spreads across Dmetri's face.

"Who? I don't know a man named Kevin. And you're early for karaoke, doesn't start until ten."

A perplexed Logan assumes Dmetri will crack a smile at any moment, revealing his joke. The smile never arrives. Logan persists.

"Kevin, the guy I was with when I met you the other night? He comes here all the time?"

Dmetri, rather than confessing a joke, appears mildly annoyed. "Sorry my friend, don't know any Kevin's."

And with that, Dmetri turns and walks away, disappearing behind the bar.

Such a strange interaction, thinks Logan. What's their game? Why the tricks? He ponders this occasionally for the next two hours, while seated in the same seat at the bar, in between vodka, beer, and anything else that is put in front of him. Eventually that familiar level of inebriation begins catching up to him, but he does his best to convince himself that he is still effective, still eavesdropping, still gathering intel.

As he stares into his phone, Logan briefly overhears a conversation between a man and a woman occurring in Russian at the opposite end of the bar. Glancing over toward the direction of the conversation, Logan sees an Eastern European male appearing to be in his mid-forties, of average height, with wavy blond hair, glasses, and a brown blazer. Seated next to him, chatting away in Russian, is an attractive younger woman with jet-black hair, pale skin, and a short red dress. The conversation is just audible enough for Logan to understand the gist of their banter.

"Po-to-mu schto, Dostoyevsky takoy skoochny! (Because Dostoyevsky is so boring!)" replies the man to his date, with a smile.

She responds, "Nyet! Eta nay pravda! (No! This is not true!)"

The rest of their conversation is drowned out by ambient noise. But something else about the pair has drawn Logan's attention. As he looks closely, he realizes there's something oddly familiar about the man. He can't quite place him. Logan's eyes struggle to focus, his vision, perhaps slightly impaired by the vodka flowing through his veins, feels confused by the strange familiarity with this man. And then it hits him. This man he stares at is Kevin. The hair is different. The glasses are new. The voice hides any evidence of an American accent. But it's Kevin. The contours of his face. His nose, his smile. Logan is sure of it. What sense can be made of this? Coming to a bar in disguise, Kevin the lothario, here to pontificate about the shortcomings of Dostoyevsky, with the ear of an eager woman?

Logan catches himself staring a bit too long and quickly looks away. He rubs his eyes, shakes his head, looks again. Not once does this impostor look over to meet Logan's gaze, which Logan can only assume is an intentional avoidance of eye contact.

"Well, this is interesting," he mumbles to himself.

A few minutes pass as Logan contemplates his next move. Should he approach? Should he initiate conversation, perhaps offer some quip about the futility of Raskolnikov's existential despair? This all sounds rather smart in his drunken mind, but the hesitation lasts for just a moment too long as Logan watches the man start to stand from his seat out of the corner of his eye. The siren with the jet-black hair remains seated.

This man, this Kevin from a parallel universe, walks toward the stairwell slowly and begins ascending the steps to the upper levels. Sensing an opportunity, Logan decides to follow. He pulls his seat back, stands, and realizes his balance is off. He grabs the bar to steady himself, keeping an eye on the Kevin impostor climbing the L-shaped stairs. Once he's steady on his feet, Logan begins to walk slowly toward the stairs, watching the man make his way past the landing in the middle of the stairwell, and past the security guard with the earpiece. Once he's certain the man is far enough ahead, Logan begins to climb the stairs. When he reaches the landing, the security guard simply steps back and allows Logan to continue without a word.

Standing at the entrance to the club room on the second floor, Logan scans the crowd. Just as before, there is an abundance of young Russian women in short skirts dancing with much older Russian men. The combination of excessively loud Russian pop music blasting from the speakers, dark lighting, and bright flashes from strobe lights is disorienting for the intoxicated Logan. Searching for a brown blazer amid all of this sensory overload, Logan spots his target, the unknown Kevin. In the corner to the right, with his back to Logan, the man approaches a red door of a darkish hue. How had Logan missed this before? A large muscular guard in a dark suit with an earpiece stands outside the door. As the man approaches, Logan watches as he pulls out a long skeleton key from the pocket of his blazer. He flashes the skeleton key to the guard, who then opens the red door and lets the man enter, closing the door behind him.

With his drunken confidence, Logan approaches the same red door, the guard eyeing him suspiciously with every forward step. Reaching into his jacket pocket, Logan gestures as if he's searching for something.

"Fuck! I think I forgot my key," proclaims Logan. "Dammit! Do you mind if I just go through, man? I won't let it happen again."

"No," replies the guard, without an ounce of empathy.

"No you don't mind, or no I can't go through?"

Logan's tone is coy, but the guardian of the red door remains unenthused.

"No."

"Listen, call downstairs if you need to. I'm a member here. I've got a key and everything."

While this had sounded convincing in his head, the charm that materializes falls far short of adequate. The guard remains stone-faced. Barring the presence of the Queen, the gravitas feels disproportionate, and Logan struggles to contain a smile. He chooses not to push his luck.

* * *

The exterior of Logan's apartment building seems relatively quiet on this particular DC night, although the presence of Christie, leaning against the building with her backpack slung over one shoulder, feels remarkably loud to Logan as his cab pulls up in front of his building. He exits and immediately begins to issue his apology, while Christie immediately recognizes that he is drunk.

"Hey, I am so sorry. I know you've probably been waiting out here for a while. My research stuff ran really late, and I—"

A frustrated Christie interrupts. "Did your research involve drinking tonight?"

"What? No…I mean, I just had a glass of beer while we were working, but I'm all good, ready to study now. Let's do it."

Her lack of patience is understandable, although Logan desperately wishes he could comfort her, soothe her, win back her good graces. She always feels the most wholesome to him during the moments when he has strayed from virtue. Alas, his bargaining is futile.

"Logan, you're drunk. I've been waiting here for twenty minutes. I don't know why I bothered. I should have known you'd show up drunk."

"What's that supposed to mean?" responds Logan defensively. "Look, if you don't want to study, that's fine, but—"

She cuts him off again. "Forget about it. I'm heading home," replies Christie indignantly, walking away in the process.

Logan makes no attempt to stop her, watching instead from a distance until he can be certain she finds her way safely back to her vehicle in the night. What a mess he can make of things, he thinks, although he knows damn well that the self-pity will become fuel for another drink once back inside. And moments later, he finds himself sitting on the couch in his living room, beverage in hand, with a movie playing on his TV that he's hardly watching. He sticks his elbows on his knees and runs his hands through his hair, staring downward, lost in thought. He picks up his phone and calls John, his old friend from the military. His motivation for doing so does not feel easily discernible in the moment, although in hindsight he will come to realize that he was desperate to experience anything other than the creeping voice of nihilism. To his surprise, John picks up.

"What's up. It's late," answers a groggy-sounding John.

"Do you ever think about it?" replies Logan.

"No."

"Sometimes I wish we were still over there."

"You alright, man?" responds a concerned John. "You don't sound alright."

"Just too much on my mind."

"You sleeping?" asks John.

"Never. You?"

"Ambien," replies a barely audible John.

"Alright, good chat," answers Logan, only partially in jest.

"Later."

Logan sets the phone down. He glances at the TV and then looks away. His leg is shaking. He cannot sit still. He picks up the phone once again, this time writing a brief text, which would receive a brief reply, which would eventually lead to an expected knock on his front door approximately one hour later.

By the time that knock arrives, Logan has cleaned himself up a bit, looking slightly more presentable for the midnight hour. He opens the front door to greet Katya, his favorite server from Bolshoi Mir. She smiles as she enters. Katya wears the same short skirt and blouse from earlier in the evening, although the skirt suddenly seems even shorter to Logan as she walks through his doorway.

"I'm glad you came," remarks Logan. "You want a drink? Some wine?"

Logan walks into the kitchen and pours two glasses of wine. Katya follows him, standing close behind him as he pours.

"I almost didn't come. Usually, if a man I meet at work invites me over to his place at midnight, I tend to assume he's got some ulterior motive."

"But you trusted mine, huh?" asks Logan.

She flashes that seductive smile once again. "Your motive? You didn't offer one. And I didn't ask."

Katya moves in closer to Logan. Before he has a chance to hand her the glass of wine, she places a hand on his back, running her fingers down his back slowly, sensually. Logan turns to face her. He brings a hand up to her cheek and brushes her hair back behind her ear. He holds the hand on her cheek and moves in for a kiss. She reciprocates. The kiss is passionate and long. Katya presses her body against Logan's. When the kiss ends, she grabs his hand and leads him to the couch, playfully pushing him over as they lie down. She presses her lips against Logan's. Moving to his neck, gently kissing, her hands running across his body. She begins to unbutton his shirt and presses her lips against his chest with every undone button. When his shirt is fully opened, she places her feet back on the floor and stands over Logan as he continues to lie on the couch. She reaches down and grabs Logan's hand, pressing it against the smooth skin of her lower leg. Keeping his hand pressed against her leg, she slowly lifts it, moving up against her inner thigh, under her skirt, between her legs. She moans in pleasure. Logan then reaches his other hand up under her skirt, and with both hands, slides her underwear down to her ankles and off her feet. With her skirt hiked up, revealing much of her inner thighs, Katya climbs on top of Logan. They embrace.

* * *

In the early afternoon of the next day, Logan is gulping down coffee at a table inside of a small café in Falls Church, Virginia. Brock and Harry sit across from him, wearing cold expressions, both with their own hands wrapped around coffee mugs, listening with skepticism to Logan's debrief. A few patrons come and go. The daylight meeting makes Logan uncomfortable, not only because of his weary vision in the sunlight or his penchant for nocturnal productivity, but because he presumes that these appointments with his handlers in such very public locales create too many opportunities for potential outside observers to wonder in peculiarity why this table of three resembles that of an insolent schoolboy sitting across from the school principals. Logan sets the paranoia aside and continues to relay the events from the night before.

"I swear, it was the weirdest thing," says Logan. "It had to have been Kevin. But why wear a disguise? And why wear it in a place you normally frequent? It doesn't make any sense."

Harry responds, "You're right, it doesn't. What were they talking about again? The guy you think was Kevin, and the woman at the bar?"

"Dostoyevsky," answers Logan.

"Dostoyevksy?"

Logan tries to explain. "Yeah, he's a writer who—"

"I know who fucking Dostoyevsky is," responds an indignant Harry.

Brock, attempting to break the tension, interjects. "Alright, so let's set aside this whole Kevin thing for a minute. Sounds like you figured out what the key is for, right? To get into some mystery room on the second floor. I want you to get one of those keys. I think you could do it, if you keep making friends. We'll try to look into this Kevin business further. Anything else from last night?"

"No," responds an exasperated Logan.

"OK good," replies Brock. "You're doing great, man. Really great stuff. I want you back there ASAP."

Logan, hoping for some sympathy, responds, "Yeah, listen, about that. I've got midterms coming up. I may have to give it a break for a couple of weeks."

"Try to get in sooner," answers Brock, rather unsympathetically. "I know you're a busy man, but it feels like we're really getting somewhere here. Just remember why you're doing it man. It's for a good cause."

CHAPTER 7

Three short nights later, Logan finds himself again sitting at the familiar bar in a now familiar routine. He listens. Drinks. Watches.

In his peripheral vision Logan spots an older, chubby, bald American male with glasses sitting at the corner of the bar. He already knows this gentleman's name is Bill, because at Bolshoi Mir, the squeaky wheel is often the loudest voice, and Bill has already proven rather boisterous. Dressed in business-casual attire, with a blazer and button-up shirt underneath, Bill drinks red wine from a large wine glass and appears to be talking out loud to no one in particular. His words are slightly slurred. Suddenly, his eyes catch Logan's gaze and he appears pleased to have a new audience.

Bill shouts to Logan from his spot in the corner.

"What are you drinking, stranger? Vodka? You have to drink red wine in a place like this. That's what Sasha likes. Sasha likes a man who drinks red wine! Don't you, Sasha?"

Sasha, the bartender, flashes Bill a smile and replies in a thick Russian accent, "Da, of course, Beelll. But I only have one favoreet customer who drinks red wine."

Bill laughs and invites Logan to join him at the end of the bar. "I'm Bill. Come on down and join me, and maybe we can make Sasha fall in love with you too."

Logan stands up, grabs his drink, and walks to the end of the bar, grabbing a seat next to Bill and introducing himself. "I'm Logan. Sounds like you know your way around this place, huh?"

"Oh yeah, I'm an irregular. A frequent attendee but far more beloved." He lets out an obnoxious, sloppy laugh, before leaning in closer to Logan and loudly whispering with a slurred voice. "You don't speak any Russian, do you? Sasha's pussy gets so wet when Americans speak Russian to her! I've slept with half the servers in this place and still haven't learned a goddamn word of Russian! Have you met Anna? Best blowjob I've ever gotten!"

Logan pretends not to be caught off guard by Bill's crassness, laughing insincerely at the drunken confessions. He briefly wonders what it must be like to operate in the world without an ounce of humility. Playing the game, he replies in a hushed tone, altering his speech just enough to appear slightly intoxicated while mirroring Bill's bravado. "Every server huh? That sounds expensive. I'm afraid I may not have the wallet to impress some of these women."

"That's nonsense!" shouts Bill. "You don't need a wallet around here. You just have to be the guy who knows the people with the wallet! Or power. Power is what will get you laid around here. Like my friends, who should be here any minute. Money and power. They could buy you and sell you ten times over…"

Bill leans in and finishes his thought in a hushed whisper to Logan. "And they could make you disappear after they do it!"

His speech returns back to its normal drunken volume as he continues. "Wait 'til you meet Oksana! She's the daughter of an oligarch, and her boyfriend Charles. Let's just say we have a mutual beneficial relationship. Hey, do you like wine? I could get you some great wine. Not here, though. But let's have a glass anyway. Hey! Speak of the devil!"

Bill's ADHD rambling is suddenly interrupted by the emerging presence of a couple in their late thirties walking through the front entrance of Bolshoi Mir. Logan senses a slight shift in energy the moment they arrive, uncertain if it's the level of physical attraction they represent or something more reputationally derived. The woman, beautiful and undoubtedly Russian, enters first. Brunette, with a tight black dress and a fur coat draped over her shoulders, she has a commanding presence. She wears her hair in a tight, stylish bun. Her sparkling earrings are expensive, and her matching necklace significantly more so. Behind her, holding the door for her, is a tall male with dark hair and a dark suit. Upon first glance, he appears American, or at least more Western than Eastern European.

Bill addresses the couple immediately. "I was starting to think you weren't going to show up. Want me to get you a drink, Oksana?"

"Hello Bill," she replies. "A glass of wine would be delightful. The party ran long—"

Her male companion interjects, "It only ran long because some retired FBI agent in attendance would not stop talking to Oksana about Moscow. We couldn't get away from him."

She smirks, replying, "Ah, Americans can be such a nuisance at events like that sometimes."

"Oksana, do you need me to pistol-whip the FBI? Get them off your back?" asks the drunken Bill obnoxiously, followed by a hearty laugh.

Oksana responds with a laugh of her own. "Oh Bill, my hero. I think we managed just fine. And now, we must celebrate!"

Bill hands Oksana a glass of wine, which she raises while making eye contact with her male companion. Bill does the same. The companion smiles and greets the gesture with a nod, placing his arm on Oksana's waist. Noticeably absent from his hand is a drink of his own. Logan, meanwhile, sits awkwardly at the bar, not yet introduced to the friends of Bill. He smiles casually at the couple before shifting his gaze elsewhere.

Bill, never one to avoid a scene, raises his glass. "To Charles! And business! And money!"

Bill takes a large gulp of his wine while Oksana lightly sips. Setting his wine glass back down on the bar, Bill turns back to Logan, commenting in a loudly staged whisper.

"Charles here just got a new contract with the NSA! Soon he'll be listening to all of our conversations!"

Charles responds coyly, "Oh Billy, you know it. You better watch out; I'll soon know the names of all those mistresses."

"I only have one mistress, and her name is Sasha!" shouts Bill in reply. "Sasha, my love, more wine please!"

Bill raises his now empty wine glass to Sasha the bartender, gesturing for a refill. Sasha smiles and rolls her eyes, grabbing Bill's wine glass and disappearing behind the bar. In this brief interlude, Logan's presence is finally acknowledged.

"Bill, you drunken fool, who is your friend?" asks Oksana. "Aren't you going to introduce us?"

She smiles at Logan, waiting for the introduction. This social nicety seems intentionally disingenuous, leaving Logan feeling even more self-conscious as a voyeuristic interloper to the affairs of this trio.

"Ah yes! This is my new friend Logan," responds Bill. "We've been enjoying the scenery together!" Bill's eyes widen as he blatantly glances around the room at all of the Russian servers.

Oksana rolls her eyes, a gesture that Bill clearly evokes in most women.

"Of course you have, Billy. It's nice to meet you, Logan. Enjoying your night?"

Logan extends his hand, shaking Oksana's hand and then briefly introducing himself to Charles with a handshake as well. "Very nice to meet you both," remarks Logan. "Bill here has been discussing the ins and outs of life in the Bolshoi Mir."

Oksana smiles in response.

"I'm sure he has. Well, as much as I wish we could stay and chat, I believe we are wanted upstairs. Have a wonderful evening, Logan."

Bill, sensing Oksana's cue, attempts to abruptly stand up from his seat. He sways clumsily, grabbing onto the bar for leverage as he stands. He turns to Logan, eager to get a final word in.

"Good luck Logan! Watch out for Sasha; she's a feisty one!"

Charles and Oksana, meanwhile, have begun moving toward the stairs that will take them to the upper levels of Bolshoi Mir. Bill drunkenly hobbles to catch up to them, like an old lapdog fearful of being forgotten. The trio disappears up the stairs, out of sight. Logan is alone at the bar once again, pondering his next move. His loneliness is short-lived, however, as Katya approaches with a smile.

"I'm on break. Join me for a smoke?" she asks.

"I'd love to."

Logan, unaware that either of them were smokers, happily follows Katya through a side door that opens into a dimly lit alley. Somehow, of all the alleys in Washington, DC, this one is free of rats, trash, and needles. Nothing but brick walls and a pretty girl. Katya hands him a cigarette and a lighter. They're both leaning with their backs against the exterior wall of Bolshoi Mir. The body language feels intimate, with their arms only inches apart and a chemistry that suggests they could pounce at any moment. They're flirting.

"So, do you always come to random Russian bars and drink alone?" asks Katya.

"Only when I think it'll improve my chances."

With a smirk and a tone of sarcasm, Katya replies, "Oh is that what it is? Just here for the women? You and Bill have so much in common."

Logan laughs. "Maybe I wanted to see you again, especially after the other night," he replies. "And, the truth is, I'm not really much of a social kind of guy. I don't keep very many friends around."

"What about a woman? Do you ever keep one of those around?"

Playing coy, he answers, "No...No. I generally just prefer meetings in dark alleys with women."

"You're terrible!" she proclaims, laughing and simultaneously gently hitting Logan's arm with a flirtatious smack.

Suddenly, in the midst of their romantic banter, a man appears out of the darkness at one end of the short alley. Appearing tall and Russian, with a long black peacoat and a shaved head, he stares for a moment, just watching them. With chiseled features and the intense gaze, he presents as a menacing figure. He begins to move, walking toward the pair down the alley.

He calls out, "Katya! There you are! I've been looking all over for you."

Katya whimpers quietly, barely loud enough for Logan to hear. She appears visibly nervous and uncomfortable. "Nikolai. Oh shit," she mutters.

"Who's this?" asks Logan quietly.

"A guy I was seeing...It's over but that hasn't seemed to register with him."

Nikolai reaches Katya and Logan, stopping only steps away from both. His gaze is fixed on Katya, making a deliberate attempt to avoid acknowledging Logan.

"Oh Katya, I told you that you must quit smoking. It will ruin this beautiful body of yours," remarks Nikolai in a thick Russian accent.

He blatantly looks Katya's body up and down slowly before continuing. "You haven't called me. I take you out for the best caviar you'll ever have, treat your body better than it's ever been treated, and you can't even bother to call me. That's no way to treat your boyfriend."

A very frustrated Katya responds, "You were never my boyfriend, Nikolai! And I told you to keep your dirty hands off my body but you couldn't take no for an answer!"

Nikolai's anger emerges just as Katya finishes her sentence. He reaches over and places both hands on her waist, pulling her toward him forcefully.

"Oh Katya, why are you trying to pretend like you're not a little slut in front of your friend here?"

Finally, Nikolai makes eye contact with Logan, flashing a cocky smile at him while his hands remain on Katya's waist. She squirms, attempting to get free from the unwanted grip.

Logan, in turn, meets Nikolai's gaze with an emotionless, cold expression. From the moment this stranger first appeared, Logan had begun mentally calculating the steps necessary to render this threat immobile. To Logan, Nikolai is nothing more than a military-aged male of above average height with a bulky jacket capable of concealing a weapon. His arm length and height would prove a disadvantage for Logan in a boxing match, but this target is all ego, desperate to intimidate. As such, his biggest blind spot would be a tendency to underestimate his enemies. As a well-dressed Russian national, presumably without any sort of diplomatic immunity, the odds are low that he would risk carrying a pistol on the streets of DC, especially with the shaved head and chiseled features. He would have a hard time disappearing into a crowd. Still, there is a nonzero chance he is armed, with a knife at the very least. Logan addresses the threat.

"She doesn't want your hands on her. I suggest you walk away and forget about her. Now."

Logan's involvement has the unintended effect of making Katya more worried, not less.

"Logan, don't worry about it. I'm fine. Go back inside," she pleads. "I'll meet you in there—"

Nikolai cuts her off. "I see your new American boyfriend is a real badass, huh? Does he know what a little slut you are?"

Nikolai keeps one hand on Katya's waist and brings the other hand up to her chin, gripping it tight. Katya is crying now. With the hand on her chin, Nikolai slowly turns Katya's head and faces her toward Logan, again making intense eye contact with him in the process. Nikolai laughs as he speaks once more. "What do you think, Mr. American Boyfriend? Is there enough of this little slut to go around?"

"This is the last warning I'm going to give you," replies Logan. "Let her go. Walk away."

"Or what?"

As he laughs, Nikolai releases Katya's chin and takes his hand off her waist. Using two fingers, he jabs them into Logan's chest, pushing him slightly and holding up his fingers afterward, staring intensely into Logan's eyes. The close proximity means he could theoretically strike at any moment. A headbutt, a knee, a right hook. Nikolai has allowed himself to get too close to pull out a blade, however. The very brief moment it would cost him to reach for a knife at such close proximity would give Logan plenty of time to neutralize the threat. Standing only inches away now, Logan realizes just how lanky Nikolai actually is. He was more imposing from a distance. Less intimidating from up close. Unpredictable, sure. But his hubris would prove to be his undoing.

"Nikolai, stop!" screams Katya. "Please! I'll have drinks with you! I'll do anything, just please stop! I don't want this! Logan, please go back inside!"

The two men ignore Katya's plea. Suddenly, in one violent gesture, Logan grabs Nikolai's outstretched arm with one hand, rolling his arm inward while using the other hand to turn Nikolai's body and slam him face-first into the wall. This is the first blow, the one that breaks his nose. A punk like this has probably had it broken numerous times before, thinks Logan. Of course, he himself is no stranger to a crooked nose. Still, there is an uncomfortable delight in seeing the blood pouring out. Before Nikolai has a chance to collect himself, Logan grabs the back of his jacket with both hands and pulls him back away from the wall while sweeping one leg behind his opponent's legs, causing him to fall over backward and land on the hard pavement with a violent thud. Concrete can make the difference between subduing and homicide, but these are thoughts for later, when vengeance fades. With Nikolai on the ground, Logan pounces on top of him, sitting upright on his knees as he begins to pummel the bloodied man in the face with the well-executed blows of a man trained to inflict maximum damage. With each clenched fist that strikes, Nikolai's face becomes a canvas of dark red slop. He gargles blood, unable to speak, each blow making the ability to assess his level of consciousness all the more challenging. There will be no tapping out, with Logan's fate and rage a little too intertwined.

Katya is in shock as she watches. She begins to scream, unable to convince her legs to start running as the horror in front of her continues for what feels like minutes. Finally, she calls out Logan's name, screaming for him to stop.

"Logan, stop! You'll kill him! Stop! Stop!"

Logan's mind is elsewhere, as if his clenched fists are driven by a primal motor beyond the realm of human decency. He isn't present. He is somewhere dark, dancing around a fire, chanting about the devil and the daylight. The violence is normal and distant. If he kills Nikolai, it will have held the same meaning as a man choosing what to eat for breakfast on a Sunday morning. Coffee, black. Eggs, scrambled. Face, mangled.

Katya continues screaming, but he hears nothing, only silence. Her mouth moves, her eyes show terror. Seconds feel like a violent purgatory.

Suddenly, Katya's screams bring him back to reality. Logan stops striking the now unconscious Nikolai's battered face. He holds his clenched fists up in front of him, watching the blood drip from his hands. With a cold, empty stare, he looks up at Katya. He remembers where he is, why he is in this alley. Abruptly, he stands, looks at Katya again, and then immediately takes off running, down the alley, around the corner, and disappearing out of her sight.

With his once professorial clothes splattered in blood, Logan now resembles a panicked madman, sprinting down the sidewalk of a posh DC neighborhood at a pace with far too much frenetic energy to be mistaken for anything other than trouble.

Lampposts light up the adjacent street with his steps, feeling at once like a spotlight and a trail of breadcrumbs back to the scene of his vicious crime. He would like to view himself as a rational, calculated creature, but in this moment he has no clue where he is going. He is not accustomed to the consequences of impulse.

Suddenly a white, unmarked van pulls up next to Logan. Two men in nondescript dark jackets and hats leap out of the vehicle and grab him. The abrupt halt feels disorienting, like a ping-ponging molecule being siphoned into an impenetrable form of containment. Logan quickly recognizes Harry, the partner of his FBI handler, as one of his captors. The other is an unknown male, silent but sturdy.

"Get in! Get the fuck in the van!" shouts Harry.

Logan is shoved inside the white van forcefully, with Harry jumping in behind him, closing the sliding door. The interior lights remain off, but the faint glow of computer monitors and surveillance equipment casts a sinister hue, like the shadow of a shadow. The engine is idling. The unknown agent hops into the driver's seat, shifts into gear, and the van peels off down the street. Harry's anger is profound and immediate.

"What the fuck are you thinking!?" yells Harry.

"I was thinking a man shouldn't lay his hands on a woman like that!" shouts a defensive Logan.

"Who fucking cares about some server! Now we can't use you at Bolshoi Mir anymore! You fucking blew it, man!"

Logan knows Harry is right about Bolshoi Mir. It is over. Maybe regret would come later, but in that moment, all he feels is contempt.

Logan responds, "Like you said, the operative word here is 'use.' Guess you can find someone else to use now."

Logan spots a half drunk bottle of water in a cup holder. He grabs for the bottle, unscrews the lid, and pours water into his hands before reaching up and scrubbing his face. The mess he makes in the van is careless, an obvious act of defiance. He quickly unbuttons his blood-spattered dress shirt that comprised his outer layer of clothing, revealing a tight V-neck undershirt. He throws the bloodied shirt on the ground in the van. While briefly stopped at a stoplight, Logan seizes the opportunity to snatch the black hat off the head of the silent van driver, quickly placing it on his own head. He throws open the van door and makes his exit, shouting to Harry as he jumps out.

"Have a nice night!"

"Go fuck yourself!" Harry responds.

* * *

By afternoon of the next day, Logan once again finds himself sitting across from Brock and Harry, the latter of whom communicates only in scowls. The three men are seated at a small square table in the back of a dive bar somewhere in Arlington. The sound of blues music plays over the speaker, with few patrons in the bar and none sitting nearby. For all of their faults, somehow the agents do have a unique ability to choose establishments that are rarely ever popular with the locals in the daylight. Logan had half assumed he would be in jail by now, and the fact that he isn't makes him wonder to whom he owes his gratitude. He relays his experiences from the night before, prior to the violence.

"So now we've got Kevin, the American from the think tank, and Bill, the drunken American banker. And they both claim to be royalty at Bolshoi Mir. And then there's Oksana, the supposed daughter of an oligarch. And Charles, who may or may not have a new job working with the NSA. Quite a cast of characters."

Brock cuts Logan off. "The NSA bit, probably just posturing. There's a lot of that in Washington. Oksana is a person of interest. Actually, they all are. But the bad news is that you fucked up. We can't use you anymore. You did good, right up until the point that you broke that dude's face in about six different locations. Thanks to us, cops are looking for a 6'2" black man weighing 220 pounds. But that won't hold for long. You better hope you didn't get caught on any cameras. But that's the last favor we can do for you. It's over. Reach under the table right now. You feel that envelope? Take it. That's the three grand we said we'd pay you."

Logan reaches under the table to grab the envelope.

Brock continues. "You'll want to keep a low profile for a little while. Keep your mouth shut. Tell no one about any of this. You won't hear from us again."

Logan doesn't know it this is true or not, and internally, he can't quite decide if he is relieved or disappointed. He craves a drink to ponder the bittersweet, but not in the company of company men.

CHAPTER 8

The crowded DC establishment emits a cacophony of drunken revelry. Pitchers of beer ebb and flow precariously from bar to table. Sports games unfold on TV screens, with the occasional patron shouting obscenities about this team or that. There are no chandeliers, no oligarchs, and no pretense, at least none currently at this table of Logan's classmates. He stands overhead, pitcher in hand, filling glasses. A pour for Laura, a stylishly dressed intoxicated mess of a doctoral candidate in her late twenties. A pour for Nathan, a comically nerdy-looking academic with perfectly boring glasses and a short-sleeve button-up tucked into wrinkled khaki pants. And finally, a pour for Christie, beautiful, shy, and exceptionally awkward. Empty shot glasses are scattered on the table. Normally Logan attempts to be more reserved with the booze among classmates he knows cannot hold their own, but to hell with caution on this night. They are all, without a doubt, rather drunk.

As Logan pours the beer into Christie's glass, his attention drifts momentarily, causing his sloppy pour to spill briefly onto Christie's lap. She laughs loudly, unfazed.

"Holy shit! I am so sorry!" shouts a genuinely embarrassed Logan.

She continues laughing. It's infectious and pure. For a brief second, the future flashes in front of him, and he hates himself for the hurt yet to come. She is low-maintenance and caring. He wants to recoil in shame, but she's too damn enchanting when she smiles.

"Don't worry about it!" replies Christie. "I don't really like these pants anyway."

Laura, sensing an opportunity for attention, adds an awkward sexual comment to address the spill. "Listen, Logan, we all know this is just a not-so-subtle attempt to get Christie out of her pants tonight."

The group laughs while Logan looks away, searching for the right words. Christie doesn't wait.

"I wish!" she blurts out impulsively. As soon as the words exit Christie's mouth, she seems to suddenly realize what she has just said, leading to her face turning bright red and a temporary silence. The rest of the group laughs again.

Nathan, fortunately interrupting the moment, remarks, "Thanks for the beer, Logan. I'll get the next round!"

"No way, man," responds Logan. "I'm buying all night! Drinks are on me! As the Russians say, 'Za zdrovya!' (Cheers to health!)"

The classmates clink beer glasses together, all smiling and appreciating the generosity, oblivious to the geopolitical tumult paying for their booze.

The rest of the night remains a bit hazy for Logan. At some point, he blinks and wakes up to the morning sun shining through the edges of the closed blinds on his bedroom windows. He is naked, under the covers of his bed, but not alone. Christie, naked and mostly asleep, slowly opens her eyes to greet him. A half-empty wine bottle and Christie's bra sit on the nightstand. Locking eyes with his, she smiles as she stretches, causing the blanket to fall slightly, partially revealing her breasts. This moment shouldn't be real, thinks Logan, as he takes a mental snapshot to keep it trapped in time.

"Good morning," says Christie. "I'm just going to go ahead and get this out of the way. You might have the most uncomfortable bed in the world."

Logan laughs and replies, "How do you feel about brunch?"

His hangover is milder than it should be. He briefly begins to wonder to himself if this is becoming a problem, pretending for a moment that the problem has not been there for months.

When he returned from war, the same three words had haunted his thoughts: drink, fuck, and fight. Drink, fuck, fight. The drinking and the fighting came easy. The romance required patience and the suppression of nihilism. On sober nights, he preferred to sleep alone, for fear that a nightmare might reveal a depravity he would rather keep to himself. How does one explain dreams of mangled intestines? Of a lost soul shouting into the blackest abyss? In war, consequences come for the just and the unjust, and the ghosts of an innocence lost emerge from every shadow, from every crowded restaurant and pile of roadside debris. It was too much to task a lover with reaching into a hell of the just-following-orders design, plucking him from all that foggy dissonance.

But now here he is, watching the sunlight hit Christie in all the right places. Drinking and fighting are both distant thoughts as he ponders satiation of a different, libidinal variety. He opts to propose brunch instead though, assuming sustenance is the more gentlemanly offer.

It takes them twenty minutes to remove themselves from the bed and throw on some clothes, and another ten to make their way a few short blocks down the street to the small café. Sitting on the same side of a wire-frame outdoor table on the patio in the sunlight, their legs touch as they both sip Bloody Marys. Coffee and half-eaten plates of food rest on the table in front of them. Neither of them can truly decide if the bright sun is a cleanser or a spotlight, but Logan can plainly tell Christie is pretending to be less hungover than she actually is.

"Do you remember what we were talking about before we both fell asleep last night?" asks Christie.

"Uh-oh," answers Logan. "Is this a test?"

Christie laughs. "No! You were talking about war. You mentioned the desert, and how beautiful the stars were at night over there. You actually told me that you wished more people would ask you about war. You…got…kind of emotional. I know it was just a drunk thing, but…you don't remember any of that?"

"Fuck, I'm sorry," responds Logan. "Sometimes that happens to me when I drink. I'm an idiot. I shouldn't be talking about that shit…Look, I really like you, but I'm obviously not in any place to be starting a relationship. There's a lot you don't know about—"

Christie cuts him off. "Stop. Don't shut down like that. I was the one who initiated things. I can make my own decisions. Don't get me wrong, I do think you drink too much, and you can be an idiot. But I don't need you to protect me. Besides, the point I was trying to make is that I liked seeing that side of you, even if we were drunk…So, tell me about war, and life, and the stars in Iraq."

Logan laughs nervously. She is unintentionally nauseating and poetic. His inclination is to stand up and flip the table over, yelling that she would never understand. The very thought, picturing himself as an insolent teenager projecting his own angst, is equally as nauseating. It is this humility that keeps him grounded and perpetually overrules the drive toward impulse, usually.

"That's a big question," remarks Logan with a smile.

Christie might sense his discomfort but has no intention of running from the topic. "Should I ask the question that I know I'm not supposed to ask?"

"Something tells me you're going to ask anyway," responds Logan. His tone is playful, at ease. It feels good to feel comfortable, he thinks to himself.

Christie asks, "Did you have to…um…" She struggles to get the wording just right.

Logan finds the attempt to be delicate rather cute and opts to help her out. "Did I have to kill anyone?"

She is embarrassed all the same. "Yeah, sorry. I should shut up," she replies.

"No, it's fine. I actually respect that someone really has the balls to ask for once."

In an overly serious tone, she looks squarely into Logan's eyes and responds, "That's me, great big balls."

They laugh together, until the moment becomes silent. The tension is gone now, but he has to dig deep in order to give her something earnest, something that he genuinely feels she rightly deserves. He looks away and stares off into another universe, diving into a sinkhole of black bile, deeper, deeper, into a cavernous abyss unknown but to him. He wrestles with an answer, a tug and pull, choking the truth and dragging it back to the surface. He holds up the head and watches the mouth move, like a puppet come to life.

"Yeah, I did. War isn't as simple as it is in the movies. It isn't just kill or be killed. I mean, it is, but it changes your perspective on life and death. Or at least it did for me. In war I learned I had the capacity to kill another human being, but not the desire. I didn't feel some internal joy when the good guys won, and I didn't feel some need for revenge when we lost. It was just one side versus the other, and fate has a way of sorting everything else out. And the moment you become complacent is the moment you become one of the unlucky ones, and sorry son, but it looks like you won't be seeing your family again. And that's the irony. You convince yourself that what you're doing is for them, and maybe it is, but they're not going to know how to talk to you when you get home anyway. It's all fucked up, I guess. You end up just feeling like some pawn in someone else's game, and—"

Logan's monologue is interrupted by the touch of Christie's lips pressed against his. The kiss brings Logan back to the present moment. Feeling a little vulnerable, he apologizes. "I'm sorry. Sometimes I can go off into my own little world."

"Don't be sorry. It means a lot to me that you'd tell me about all of that. How did you stay sane? I mean, I don't think I could do it. I know I couldn't."

Logan takes a bite of his cold eggs, buying himself some time as he ponders the question.

"Well, I'll tell you a little secret that I've never told anyone before. About midway through my deployment, I bought a copy of this outdoors magazine. You know, best places to hike and all that. Well, one day, after a particularly tough mission, I'm flipping through the magazine, and in the back, where all the little ads are, is a real small tourist ad for a tiny little mountain town in Wyoming, called Big Horn. I didn't know anything about this town, had never heard of it. But there's this picture of the Big Horn main street, and it's literally just a post office and a bar, and some little restaurant. And in the background, rising up into the skyline, are these beautiful, mind-blowing mountains. So I see this ad, and I can't stop staring. I rip it out of the page, and I tape it to this cabinet in my little hut next to my bed. And every day I just stare at it. I become obsessed with this town, Big Horn. I start reading all the history, learning everything I can. And that's how I stayed sane. Big Horn, Wyoming."

"So did you ever go? When you got back?" Christie asks.

"No. I never got the chance. Nine days after I got out of the military, I started grad school. And here I am."

Christie pauses for a moment, her facial expression turning to temporary concern, as she considers this delay in destiny.

"Well, I hope you'll go someday, after all this," she answers.

* * *

Approximately two months later, alone and asleep in his bed at 5 a.m., Logan is startled awake by the sound of his phone ringing. Bolting upright, he's sweating, confused, disoriented from the demons of his dreams. The phone rings again, sounding particularly thunderous as he gathers his bearings. He glances over and sees Unknown Caller on the screen. Answering his phone is typically a task he finds particularly aversive, but something unknown compels him to answer, as if pressured by his own intuition.

"Hello? Who is this?" he speaks into the phone; it's too early for niceties.

"Logan, it's Brock. I've got something for you. It's urgent. I need you to meet me ASAP."

"When?"

"Right now. I'm outside your building, parked two blocks down, right hand side, Park Road. Blue Crown Vic. Leave your phone."

"I'll be out in a minute," Logan responds without hesitation.

Throwing the covers off himself, he stands and searches for a pair of jeans off his floor, followed by a black hoodie. He is groggy and yet the movements feel automatic, as if he didn't have a choice in any of this. He grabs a compact folded knife off his dresser. The blade is small but the release is quick. This is his everyday carry, his most effective tool. He steps into a pair of tennis shoes without tying the laces and throws his hood over his head before making his way out of the bedroom. Someday, he would feel ashamed that his unconscious mind could generate so much enthusiasm for his probable demise.

As he walks down the sidewalk of a dimly lit DC street outside his townhouse building, his hood is pulled up and his gaze, to the outside observer, appears focused on the ground in front of each step. He is acutely aware of his surroundings however, cautious enough to keep one of the hands in his jean pockets gripped around the knife, ready to pull it out if needed. Approaching a parked, nondescript Crown Vic, he glances up to see only one passenger sitting in the darkness on the driver side. Logan moves to the passenger side door and opens it, sliding inside quickly. The interior lights of the car remain off.

Brock greets Logan with a handshake and an insincere smile. There must be a sales pitch coming, Logan imagines. Some reason why Brock would wake him in the early morning hours to feign authenticity.

"Hey, brother, long time no see. Sorry to wake you, man," says Brock.

"What's up?"

"I've got good news and bad news," responds Brock. "Bad news is it turns out your little fight in the alley a couple months ago was caught on camera."

"Damn. Security camera? So what's the good news?"

"Good news is we made it disappear. You don't have to worry about it. But I need something from you. Actually, the Bureau needs your help with something. I know it's last minute, very last minute. But it will be huge for US government."

"I'm listening," responds a curious Logan.

"There's a Russian agent, a diplomat. Works in cyber defense for the Russian Embassy. He travels a lot, around the US, in and out of the country, going to different consulates, doing IT shit. Listen, I'm gonna spare you many of the details, because this is a need-to-know type of situation. But these cyber defense guys, they're often linked to the GRU and the FSB. Real masters of their craft. Valuable assets for the Russians. Do you remember that story a couple years ago about Russian hackers shutting down a water treatment facility in Mississippi? You probably heard all the talk about the need to protect critical infrastructure projects?"

Logan nods and listens, waiting for the punchline.

Brock continues. "Well, here's a thing that you probably never heard. So they make this water tank overflow in this small town in Mississippi, OK, could be bad, but what's the big deal, right? Well this wasn't an immediate fix. The town had to shut off water flow to all buildings, all residents living within city limits, for about four hours. Well it just so happens that on that exact same day, we had a defector, a source from inside Russian intelligence that we had managed to recruit, who we were keeping in hiding until we could get him safe and secure. I cannot stress enough how valuable this individual was for us. Never in my entire career have I seen the Bureau be so incredibly careful about protecting the identity of a source like this. I mean, there was some real paranoia around this. Only a few people working the case actually knew the identity of the source, and only a few, three to be exact, knew where the asset was being hidden while we did the vetting and prepared a new life for him.

"The agents working that case, they trusted no one. No one. So what do they do? They get their defector and hole him up in a shitty hotel in the middle of nowhere, rural America, the kind of place Russian intelligence services couldn't go anywhere near without drawing suspicion. And where was this? Small-town Mississippi. The same small town where the water treatment facility gets shut down, where the town loses water for nearly four hours. Well during those four hours, the asset is in this rundown hotel room with one agent inside and one in the parking lot watching the perimeter. Suddenly, there's a knock at the hotel room door. The dude working the front desk at the hotel, Indian fella, young, is holding a package, a small box that he says was dropped off at the front desk with instructions to deliver to Room 207, the very room with the agent and the asset. Now, this is small-town Mississippi, there's no local bomb squad, nobody that's gonna test for anthrax. The agent has to think fast.

"Do they blow their cover and risk the exposure? He makes a judgment call. If the package is indeed coming from somewhere nefarious, he assumes that the Russians wouldn't risk such an obvious assassination of an American agent on US soil, so he takes the package, walks to the far corner of the parking lot alone, box in hand, sets it on the ground, kneels down, and opens it—cautiously. Not the decision I would have made, but to each their own. Anyway, nothing blows up. No white powder in his face. Instead, there's a card and three bottles of water inside. He opens the card and the message is addressed to the defector and the full names of both FBI agents. All it says is, 'We thought the three of you could use some water today. Enjoy. Courtesy of the Russian Embassy.'

"So you see, when the opportunity arises to get a glimpse into how these units operate, we have to take it. And that's what we have right now. An opportunity. This diplomat I mentioned, in cyber defense, guys like this don't ever, ever, travel alone. Usually there's a security detail, someone watching them. Making sure there's never a chance they might get recruited and pass along some IT secrets to guys like me. Well, we've managed to stumble upon an incredibly rare, golden opportunity. Turns out our boy has had to change some travel plans and is catching a last-minute flight from Dallas to DC. And guess what? The flight was too booked for that security detail to travel with him."

Logan, getting impatient, asks, "And you want me to meet him? Where? In Texas? In DC? At the airport?"

"Oh no, my friend," responds Brock. "We want you sitting in the seat right next to him for the entire three-hour flight."

"I thought it was booked?" asks a confused Logan.

"It is. And one of those seats is reserved for you."

"When?"

"I need you in Dallas at 7 p.m. tonight," answers Brock. "And you'll be catching the flight back to DC tomorrow morning, ready to learn all kinds of new things about the man sitting next to you on that plane…So what do you say? You're a patriot, right?"

CHAPTER 9

Dallas Fort Worth International Airport. 7:02 p.m. CST.

Logan stands alone outside of the airport, waiting at the pickup point for arrivals. His instructions are minimal. The red car will pick you up. Tom will be the driver. Tom wears glasses. Carry your backpack over your right shoulder. Wear your blue George Washington University baseball cap. Look for the red car.

Logan wears the hat pulled low over his eyes. His nerves make his hands want to shake, but he won't allow it. In an unconscious effort to seem calm, he overcompensates and appears a little too stoic as he stands and waits. This is not casual conversation among the fur coats and the short skirts. His mission is not that of a transcribing voyeur or a drunken flirt. This feels operational, an elevation in responsibility, the confluence of the tactical and the strategic. He knows the consequences of fucking up would feel detrimental to something greater than himself. Although Logan tries to pretend otherwise, underneath the layers of a dozen defenses exists a desperation for validation, a deep desire to prove his value, to make his country proud.

A red sedan pulls up and Logan opens the passenger door, abruptly taking a seat. Tom, a heavyset FBI agent with short, buzzed blondish hair and glasses, sits behind the wheel. In contrast with his passenger's restraint, Tom is immediately energetic and talkative. He greets Logan with an enthusiastic handshake and then quickly hands him a manila envelope before driving off.

"Hey, I'm Tom. Welcome to the big time!"

Logan instantly assesses Tom as comically disingenuous, confusingly so. How many times has some naïve schlub sat in this same seat, he wonders. How many confidential human sources, how many cosplay James Bonds, are enchanted by the patronizing whims of a chubby fellow with a badge masquerading as something cloak and dagger? These fleeting thoughts help Logan to relax, to ease up. Find the humor, he thinks, and he'll get through this quickly.

"Info about the target is in this envelope," continues Tom. "You'll find a picture of him in there too."

Logan opens the envelope, pulling out a piece of paper with writing on it and a picture. He reads the name of the target out loud.

"Mikhail Ivanov."

"Yep, that's our guy," replies Tom.

"Married? Kids? What do we know about him?" asks Logan.

"I think the less you know about the target going into the situation, the better. It'll help the conversation go a bit more smoothly if you're learning things about him as you chat."

Logan finds this answer less than satisfactory.

"Is this your way of telling me you guys don't actually know anything about this dude? What happens if he falls asleep as soon as he sits down? Or maybe he puts headphones in right away? Surely I'm not alone in considering all these variables?"

Tom replies, "Let's strategize about the approach when we get to the hotel. I got a bottle of bourbon waiting for you. How's that for a plan?"

The drive to the hotel is another twenty minutes, which Tom spends attempting lighthearted small talk about travel and bourbon and TV shows. Logan assumes this fluff is meant to serve the dual purposes of making a source feel comfortable while simultaneously attempting to assess their readiness. Perhaps, though, this is giving Tom too much credit.

The two men finally arrive at an upscale hotel in downtown Dallas. The lobby is quiet, with soft lighting, faint jazz music, and cucumber water. Logan wonders what name the room is under. Why stay somewhere with class? He is, after all, being asked to play some version of himself—doctoral candidate, researcher, Russian-speaking counterterrorism expert, war veteran with a slight drinking habit, broke graduate student. None of this screams out disposable income. He adds it to the list of peculiarities, of unanswered questions for the glorified boys in blue.

Tom had checked into the room long before Logan's arrival. As promised, the bourbon is waiting on a small table positioned between two cushioned chairs placed at angles toward the bottle. Even the lighting in the room seems to prefer the bourbon as the focal point. Logan silently finds humor in the idea that chubby Tom had been in this room hours before, strategically placing furniture and mapping out the evening. It all feels so very deliberate, so strangely contrived, like a tourist walking onto an Agatha Christie play. Tom immediately grabs the ice bucket and says he'll be back as he invites Logan to have a seat. Moments later he returns, ice in hand, and fills up two lowball glasses with the ice and the bourbon. Logan cannot tell if Tom is either eager for the drink or eager to get on with the night so that he can make his way home, wherever that might be.

"Now remember," says Tom, "You were in Dallas for the psychology convention. You're finishing up your doctorate in DC. That part's true, obviously, so you shouldn't fuck that up. But don't come on too strongly. You want to seem friendly but not pushy."

"Is there a psychology convention?" asks Logan.

"I don't know. He won't ask. Listen, don't offer any excess information voluntarily. You learn that at Quantico pretty early on. The school was different back then, pre-9/11. Damn I'm getting old! But anyway, that's one thing that hasn't changed. People don't talk that way naturally. They don't casually offer exposition. Learn what you can about him, but it's gotta come naturally. I can't stress that enough, be natural. Be agreeable, but not obvious. Make sure you find a way to pass along your business card to him. If he wants to grab a drink later tomorrow night, you do it. I don't care if the guy wants you to meet up with him and go pick up some hookers in Chinatown. You do it. But if none of that happens, and all you get is whatever you get during the flight, this is the address where you'll meet Brock afterward."

Tom hands Logan a small slip of paper with a restaurant name and address on it. *Irish Tavern. 6400 Biloxi Road. Bethesda, Maryland.*

"You know the place?" Tom asks.

"I've heard of it," Logan responds.

"Well, hopefully you'll never see it because you'll be too busy snorting lines off a stripper's ass with your new Russian friend."

Hookers, strippers, cocaine. The whiskey. The nice hotel. Does this shit actually work, wonders Logan? How many times has Tom buttered up some lackey before sending him into the lion's den of Russian intelligence? If the Bureau wants to catch Ivanov in a compromising position, perhaps sending a graduate student to get him from point A to point B is a misguided exercise in futility. Or perhaps the alcohol-infused Tom is inadvertently showing the Bureau's cards and revealing a weak hand.

"But like I said," Tom continues, "it's a win if you give him your card, and if that's that, you'll get a cab. Brock will be at the restaurant waiting for you. Now, you can't keep that slip of paper. Copy down the address in your own handwriting. We can't take any chances."

Logan grabs a pen and pad of paper from the desk in the room and begins copying down the address. There are moments when they're thorough, and there are moments when they're cavalier. Perhaps, thinks Logan, the trick is to avoid ever becoming expendable.

Eventually, the whiskey begins to run low and Tom leaves, but not before he utters once more to give Ivanov that damn business card. As Tom exits the room, closing the hotel room door behind him, the room suddenly feels strangely quiet to Logan. He is left to ruminate, with the vociferous voice in his head detailing the one hundred ways this whole operation might go south. It all seems a bit haphazard, as if Logan's handlers care only about the opportunity, with little concern for any of the risk. They want Logan to believe he has a get-out-of-jail-free card, a waiver for any trouble he might find himself in while he protects democracy one dastardly deed at a time. The problem with taking on a role in which he plays a slightly more wayward version of himself is that all the exposure will perpetually be his burden to bear. He has a growing sense of discomfort with all of this, with knowing that his loyalty is once again becoming the ultimate temptation of fate.

He sleeps very little that night, struggling to find the exit sign from his own mind. The dark circles under his eyes visible in the light of the next morning are already a permanent fixture on his face, and thus there is nothing amiss in his sleep-deprived fashion. He sits in silence on the shuttle ride to the airport, and he sits alone and silent in the crowded terminal once he arrives at his gate. He had only been shown the one picture of Mikhail Ivanov, which for obvious reasons he was not allowed to keep. While he had been informed this was indeed a recent photograph, this singular picture committed to his memory feels inadequate as he occasionally glances around and attempts to sift through the thousand busy faces in his purview. Fortunately, people watching is a favorite hobby of airport enthusiasts, so he never looks out of place with his subtle scanning, but he still makes a conscious effort to read the news on his phone.

Time is moving quickly now, and boarding will begin in approximately ten minutes. How humorous, but grossly disappointing, would all of this be if the target fails to show up, thinks Logan. All of the lost sleep, the lost hours, and the expended cortisol, only for a no-show. But this is a fairly complex operation, with a number of moving parts that has to line up perfectly just for one man to sit next to another. Logan has faith that the logistical challenges have been accounted for, that his handlers would not be so cavalier as to design a scenario in which they blew an opportunity of such magnitude. He is wrong.

The boarding agent announces boarding is about to begin, but there is no Mikhail Ivanov in sight. Because Ivanov has priority boarding, Logan has priority boarding. This puts him in a precarious position. He might have to board before he has any evidence that Ivanov will follow. Getting off the plane once he is already on will undoubtedly arouse far more suspicion than not getting on at all. Boarding begins and still no target. Logan goes through the motions, standing and moving toward the line, trying not to sweat, trying not to be too obvious while he minds his peripheral vision. He inches closer in line, growing more uncertain with each step as to whether he should proceed with boarding. He feels ill-prepared for this situation. The gate attendant is a larger woman with an eagle eye, diligently working to keep the line speedy and uniform. Logan exercises autonomy and makes a call. He chooses to step out of line, just off to the side, and pretends to rummage through his bag, hopefully buying himself some time. While he searches in haste for an unknown item, his phone suddenly rings. Logan answers, and the voice of Tom begins speaking with urgency.

"Abort. Abort. Go around," says Tom.

"Roger," replies Logan.

He quickly zips up his bag and begins walking speedily through the airport, choosing not to look back at his gate. He is swift but calm, exiting the cleared side of the airport, past the baggage claim, outside to the passenger pickup, where Tom is already waiting in the red sedan. Logan hops in and Tom immediately drives off.

"What happened?" Logan asks. "No-show?"

Tom replies, "He pushed his flight back a day. He's in Dallas still, but leaving tomorrow morning now. You'll be on tomorrow's flight with him."

"Does he know?" asks Logan. "Is that what this is about? Him learning it wasn't safe? Won't it be obvious that I've rescheduled my own flight?"

"Look, we're monitoring all web traffic to the airline. No obvious anomalies. People change their flights all the time."

"And his security detail? Will he be watched? Guarded?" asks Logan.

"Again, no obvious anomalies. None of the names on our radar are popping up. We'll get you sitting next to him. All you gotta do is work your charm. Nothing else matters," responds Tom.

Logan can sense the frustration in his voice and on his face. This is Tom without the fluff, curt and lapidarian in his replies. He has the appearance of a man who has been awake since the middle of the night, juggling stressors to which Logan had not been privy. The operation has perhaps grown more complicated, Logan thinks. Surely there is someplace Tom would rather be. He doesn't wear a ring, but there is an indent and tan line on the finger where his ring should be. He hasn't mentioned kids, but Logan notices a sprinkle of glitter near the ankle of his right pant leg. Tom is most likely a family man, a fact which he has chosen to conceal from Logan. And the red sedan Logan is riding in is too clean for either a family man or a chubby single male, suggesting this is a company car. Given that Tom is flustered, heavyset, and less interested today in buttering up their confidential human source, Logan surmised this is a man whose blood pressure runs high and whose tolerance for deviation runs low.

"We're heading back to the same hotel," says Tom. "Not the same room, though. It's your lucky day. All they had left were suites at the top. We paid to have the room ready early. Under your name. Rest up, watch TV, jerk off, whatever you want to do. The restaurant downstairs has good food. Get yourself a steak tonight and have a few drinks at the bar. But whatever you do, be ready to go tomorrow morning at 8 a.m. Stay out of trouble. Don't reek of booze. Be ready to go in the morning. Got it?"

"Roger that," replies Logan.

Tom drops Logan off in the parking lot at the side of the hotel, choosing not to pull directly in front of the lobby. This time, there will be no complimentary bottle of bourbon, no attempts on the part of Tom to make sure Logan is relaxed and comfortable. Both men seemingly prefer it this way. Just as Tom is eager to return to an unmentioned life, Logan is looking forward to time spent alone without watching and being watched, without the tension of a poor man's tradecraft.

Logan walks across the parking lot and steps into the lobby with the jazz and the cucumber water. As much as he wishes he could keep his head down and avoid eye contact, the room is under his name and a room key will be needed. He steps in front of the check-in desk to find no one around at this late morning hour. There is a bell to ring, but he imagines that the sound of it will feel rather aggressive, not to any hotel employees but to his tired brain.

Logan had once spent time in Iraq at a base known affectionately as "Mortaritaville," and proximity to mortar rounds had left a perpetual ringing in his ears that was greatly exacerbated by sleep deficits, stress, and loud noises. So the bell is thus something he would prefer to avoid, opting instead to stand in silence with his head bowed, assuming that some camera will alert someone in a back room that a hotel guest is waiting. Instead, a short, bubbly, and ponytail-adorned hotel employee with a name tag bearing the name Stacy comes rounding a corner behind the desk, mindlessly attending to some checklist and oblivious to the silent man in waiting.

"Oh my!" she proclaims, stepping back frightened at the unexpected sight of Logan. "I'm so sorry! I didn't see you there. I was in my own little world and you're so quiet up here! Good morning. How can I help you?"

"Morning," responds Logan, dryly but pleasant enough. "I'm checking in. I should have a suite reserved."

"Oh, well it's actually rather early for check-ins," responds Stacy, very matter-of-factly.

Logan smiles with an insincere degree of patience and states, "I understand, Stacy. But the room is already paid for, already reserved, and already available. I'm guessing if you search under the name Callahan, you'll find a suite eagerly waiting for my presence."

Stacy quietly types the name into the computer before looking up and flashing a disingenuous smile, stating, "I'll just need to make a copy of your driver's license."

"Of course," replies Logan.

As Stacy disappears to make the copy, Logan glances over at the hotel restaurant. A steakhouse with a long, slender, attractive bar. Stacy returns and acknowledges Logan's interest.

"I see you found Ottavino, our James Beard Award–winning steakhouse!" She is excited once again and continues, "The restaurant opens at 5 p.m. I would highly recommend the bone-in ribeye. They do this really wonderful smoked Jalisco rub that—"

Logan cuts her off, asking, "And what time does the bar open, Stacy?"

"It opens at 3 p.m., sir," she responds, handing him his room key.

"Wonderful. You take care, Stacy."

The room is spacious enough, as promised, but not big enough for Logan to run from his own thoughts. He could try to sleep, but he knows he wouldn't. He could work on his clinical notes for his doctoral program, but he is a spy waiting to meet a spy in a hotel suite in Texas paid for by the FBI. Everything is bound to feel a little mundane in comparison. He is growing increasingly troubled by this, though, by the fact that adrenaline is beginning to make the ordinary intolerable.

While he has been forever in search of stillness, he remains just as terrified of finding it. Logan is insufficiently prepared for a multiday excursion, so he does what he can to freshen up his clothes and largely avoids wearing them. He spends the afternoon reading, practicing his Russian, and rehearsing an approach to Ivanov. He counts the hours until the bar opens. He will have a few drinks, order dinner, and then perhaps have a few more before calling it a night. Stacy had suggested the steak, and why not? It isn't his budget.

The bar might have opened at three but Logan is proud of himself for having the willpower to hold off until four. He doesn't want to appear too eager, after all. Much to his dismay, there is a group of five alleged financial analysts already occupying seats at the bar downstairs, appropriately sporting the Oxford cloth and the requisite outdoorsy fleece vest rarely worn by anyone in the outdoors. Logan finds himself the seat farthest away. The group is already loud, already ordering shots, already planning out their eighteen holes for the next day. If he is being honest with himself, Logan is almost envious of their energy. They are roughly the same age as he, but they seem so young and he feels so old.

Logan orders his whiskey on the rocks, which is fortunately made quickly, and suddenly life seems tolerable. The bar itself is lacking in stimulation, but he tells himself he is just happy to be here. A poem runs on loop through his mind, as they often do. Today it is Robert Frost reminding him of his responsibilities and the many miles left before he can be free of them. He is ashamed that he needs to be so deliberate in his actions as to require a conscious effort to behave himself. He is successful initially, and his efforts remain untested until the finance bros begin buying rounds for the entire bar, of which Logan is the sole additional patron. Thus, he has to partake in shots of a cinnamon-flavored whiskey, which then requires partaking in the expression of gratitude and exchange of niceties. He has no intention of buying anyone a drink himself, but his new friends do not seem to mind.

"What brings you to Dallas?" The ringleader asks Logan from across the bar.

It might be socially appropriate for Logan to relocate closer to the group providing the free drinks, but he is quite content and remains in his seat.

"I was just visiting for a psychology convention, nothing terribly exciting. How about you guys?"

The man reacts loudly, and perhaps a little drunkenly, without actually responding to Logan's question.

"Whoa! A psychiatry convention! Well, I think all my boys here could use some meds!"

The entire group laughs in a manner that would have felt forced in sober circumstances.

Logan, quite used to the confusion between psychology and psychiatry, chooses not to correct him, instead responding, "Well for now, I think we all have the best medicine right here." He smiles and raises the shot glass before adding, "Cheers."

"Cheers!" responds the group of men in unison, and the cinnamon concoctions disappear.

This continues for two more rounds. Logan, for his part, is pleased to have found new friends who ask for absolutely nothing in return. In fact, the group seems to practically revel in its ability to contribute to the intoxication of others. But as the laughs and the cheers persist, something ethereal is silently gliding in, through the lobby, through the restaurant, and right up to the bar. She sits one seat apart from Logan. Her presence immediately silences the boisterous lot, as if they suddenly find themselves staring at an angel in such awe that prostration could be their only logical step to follow. She appears to be of South Asian ethnicity. Beautiful but silent, she acknowledges absolutely no one but the bartender at the moment. She wears a green dress that is tight and short and speaks the same language as Logan. She orders her whiskey neat. She has all the little devils furiously turning cogs in the recesses of Logan's mind. She is intimidating before she ever glances in his direction and he knows he had to say something, anything.

"So, you prefer to drink it neat, huh?" asks Logan. "I respect that. I would love to get your next one if you'll allow me."

"No thank you," she replies coldly, without remotely looking in his direction.

"Well, enjoy your night then," responds Logan.

"So that's all it takes?" she asks, finally turning to meet his eyes with her own. "An ounce of defeat and you tuck your tail between your legs?"

Logan responds, "Well, if you've already assumed I'm a dog from the start, then I suppose everything else is pretty futile at this point."

She laughs and replies, "Well, perhaps not a dog, but a little bird desperate for a branch to land on. Unfortunately for you, it won't be on my tree, though."

She smirks as she holds up her left hand to flash a wedding ring.

"And yet here you are," answers Logan, "alone at a hotel bar, ordering your whiskey neat, wearing that dress."

"Oh, I'm sorry," she replies sarcastically. "You'd prefer I not be seen? Or perhaps stay covered in public? Shall I return back to my room and grab my hijab? Please. I thought I left men like you behind in another lifetime."

"Men like me?" questions Logan. "You mean respectful men who happen to notice when a beautiful woman sits next to them?" Logan is flustered, uncertain as to how to proceed. Part of him wants to turn his back to her, to ignore her. He finds himself far too exhausted to accept the drama, and to compete with the wit. But the other part of him was locked under her spell the moment her eyes locked onto his. His intuition is telling him to run away, while the rest of him says to stay and accept the beating.

"You're smooth, aren't you?" she replies.

"Am I?"

She turns her gaze to address the bartender. "Tommy, please put the next and final round for my new friend here on my bill," she says.

To Logan, she is simply the woman in the green dress. He feels pulled toward her, as if some inexplicable magnetic force needs him to know that her presence will come to matter, someday if not now. Her real name is Zafirah. Born in Lahore, Pakistan, she immigrated to the United States with her mother at the age of eight. Her mother had been a brilliant woman, but she had the misfortune of being married to a man from a narrow societal class that had no use for a woman's intellect. Zafirah's father had owned and operated a local carpet manufacturing business, which sustained the family but allowed for very little luxury. There was wealth in Lahore, but he had never known it. He was a notoriously miserable man. Zafirah's mother often absorbed the brunt of that misery. He could be violent, which her father hid behind the veil of "traditionalism." Zafirah was fortunately naïve enough during her childhood to believe that hers was ideal. And she lived this way until her mother's health started to change shortly after Zafirah turned eight.

At first, she just seemed a little weak. Some exhaustion, some coughing. But then the bruises started to appear around her chest. She tried to hide it from Zafirah, who assumed the bruising was caused by her father anyway. Eventually though, doctors would diagnose her mother's symptoms as primary angiosarcoma of the breast. She had cancer, an extremely rare and aggressive form that required immediate treatment with surgery and likely chemotherapy. Without taking urgent action, the possibility of death would remain high. Even with treatment, the odds were unfavorable. But Zafirah's mother was a strong woman and she intended to fight, not least because she was terrified at the prospect of leaving Zafirah alone to grow up with a father who was anything but warm. Lahore had cancer centers, including a brand-new facility only four blocks from the family's home. Ease of access to treatment would have been a nonissue, if only her husband had allowed for it. The cancer center unfortunately was funded by western NGOs, and her husband refused to allow his wife to get the help she needed. Months passed and her condition worsened to the point that her prognosis was all she had left to hide from her daughter. But as the situation became more dire, her desperation turned to resourcefulness, and one day while her husband was working, she scooped up her daughter and climbed into the back of a vehicle arranged by an NGO to pick them up and drive them to the airport, where they would eventually fly to America and leave Lahore behind. In the US, Zafirah's mother was evaluated quickly at a prestigious hospital in Baltimore. Her cancer was so rare that the oncologists excitedly treated her as a case study. Unfortunately, their enthusiasm was not enough to salvage the odds and give Zafirah more time with her mother.

Four months after arriving in America, her mother died. Zafirah was alone, having been transported in a whirlwind from the bustling streets of Lahore to the bustling streets of Baltimore. Before her death, her mother had taken steps to ensure Zafirah could be adopted by an American family and remain in America. She may have taken some liberties with the paperwork when she suggested that Zafirah would have no home to return to back in Pakistan. And thus, at eight years old, in the midst of her grief, her loneliness, and her fear, little Zafirah began learning how to become an American, eventually spending her formative adolescent years straddling the line between memories of Lahore and the ambitions of a western education. She was beautiful and intelligent. She was her mother's daughter. In her twenties, at the advice of a physician, she chose to preemptively get a double mastectomy to minimize any cancer risk to herself. She was rather proud of the breast implants she received in return, and she regarded them as a valuable weapon in her arsenal as a contractor for the Federal Bureau of Investigation. Zafirah had been recruited while pursuing her undergraduate degree in international relations, the pursuit of which she was finding to be absurdly expensive. But as a beautiful dark-skinned American woman with language fluency in Punjabi and Urdu, she was exactly the kind of asset that the FBI desired to have on their payroll. Suddenly, college was an expense she needn't worry about. Promises were made, of course, about how helpful she could be in preventing attacks motivated by radical Islamic extremism.

This was a thrill she had longed for. On a deeper subconscious level, this was an opportunity to bring down men like her father, whom she had grown to blame for her mother's death. And for the first few years, this was exactly what she had done. She had a skill for convincing men to hand over information they never dreamed of handing over. She could cite Islamic scholars in Urdu among a group of hard-liners, but as long as she wore the right dress, they would all deviate from their faith in a heartbeat. Zafirah was uncompromisingly fierce though, and she developed a reputation within the Bureau for being difficult, for being anything but a team player. After years of her supervisors encountering what they characterized as drama, they had begun sending her on assignments selected based only on the criterion that they could minimize interactions with her. And thus, she went from assisting in counterterrorism to, as she put it, "babysitting" an entitled American war veteran who had a propensity for drinking too much and sometimes himself opting to go a little rogue. Her only mission was to ensure Logan returned to his own hotel room that night. She had little patience for anything else.

Logan, still simultaneously confused and mesmerized, replies, "Well that's very generous of you, but is it my final round?" He smiles and tries to mask his excitement, internally wondering what comes next and silently hoping it's moving on somewhere with her. He adds, "And you never actually told me what brings you here."

"I'm not sure you ever really asked," she replies. "But if you must know, I'm just here to make sure little birdies fly back to their nests at the end of the night."

She holds her gaze just a few seconds longer than is necessary for emphasis.

A wave of sudden embarrassment silences Logan as he realizes that a babysitter had been sent to keep him from wandering off for the evening. Those bastards, he thinks. He's the one risking all the exposure and yet they pull stunts like this? He is filled with anger, with scorn, a fair amount of which is directed toward the self. He has a distinct feeling that someday he might see this woman in green again, but he has no interest in seeing her any further while on his present journey. She has left his ego wounded, although the deeper wound is in the recognition that someone felt she needed to be sent in the first place. Logan stands and mumbles to himself, "I think I'll have that steak in my room." And with that, he walks toward the elevator without saying another word. Zafirah makes no attempt to stop him. She sips on her whiskey and smiles, seemingly pleased with herself.

Before he steps into the elevator Logan chooses to look back once more at the woman in green. She had toyed with him, left him feeling foolish. He wants nothing and everything to do with her. The elevator doors close behind him. Perhaps he'll solve that mystery on some other night in some other town.

Later that night, back in his hotel room, Logan's sleep proves to be disjointed at best. He has dreadful dreams of storms on a distant and dusty horizon, of lightning approaching across a vast desert landscape that is too big for him to comprehend but too small for him to have room to run. He dreams of a massive dust storm he once encountered during a deployment to Iraq, a storm known in the Arabic language as a haboob, that once moved in slow motion toward his desert base and the skeleton crew that occupied it, a menacing storm that crept in from somewhere far and barren, sweeping over the dens of jackals, the old huts, and the MiG graveyards strewn among dilapidated airfields. The storm promised to swallow Logan and his compatriots whole, and indeed its arrival brought such a thick cloud of sand and dust that the sunlight left early that day and all that remained was sand piled into every corner of every structure. He dreams of impending doom and awakes thirty-five minutes before his alarm with an uneasy feeling that he is in a passenger seat being driven by a fate that refuses to use headlights in the dark. But he is a man of conviction, he tells himself, and he will again honor this commitment of service before self, even if his intuition tells him to run and leave all this absurdism behind. He needs to feel like he is a part of something greater, which is why he is early that morning as he stands waiting in the parking lot for Tom, while Tom himself arrives right on schedule.

As they speed off, Logan's thoughts are quite adamant that he will never see that hotel again. He mentions the babysitter to Tom in a disgruntled tone but receives only a reply of feigned ignorance. The drive is mostly silent. Once at the airport, Logan passes through security without issue and finds his gate, once again sitting and waiting for a target that has yet to emerge. If the target fails to show and he is asked to repeat this process all over again, he will immediately assume that he is actually an unwitting participant in some sort of Kafkaesque experiment. He imagines a man and his colleagues on the other side of a two-way mirror laughing at him, at the number of times they can make him repeat these steps. As such, he vows to himself that he will board this flight, with or without the target seated next to him. And for a moment, it seems this very scenario may come to fruition. Boarding is about to begin. The target has not arrived. No Russians in sight. Logan is getting on this damn plane. But then, he appears.

Of average height, with unmistakably Eastern European facial features, Mikhail Ivanov presents as stoic and calm. This is not a flustered man who barely made his gate. His presence in a crowd could easily be overlooked. His short, graying hair with a widow's peak and larger forehead make his age somewhat ambiguous. Dressed in business-casual clothing with a tan blazer, he carries a black laptop bag slung over his shoulder. He is alone, or at least he appears to be. Everything about him is so perfectly unremarkable, to the point of frustration for Logan. He wants Ivanov to be a man who owns his environment, a man who wears a propensity for intellectual wit in his physical posture. But this is rather disarming instead. Logan is relieved to spot Ivanov but takes care not to draw any attention to himself with his gaze.

The gate attendant announces that boarding can begin for the flight. Logan stands and walks toward the line. His internal monologue is all the while engaged in a shouting match. "Be cool! Don't tremble! Don't overcompensate by looking stiff. Don't smile too much. Don't scowl." The internal never manifests as external. The line moves, and Logan himself is perfectly unremarkable within it.

As Logan walks through the tunnel, boarding the plane, it all feels very fast. Ivanov is farther back, not yet boarding. Ivanov would have the window and Logan would have the aisle, with no middle seat. Although this would be an exit row, the economy seating would still mean close quarters. The benefit of arriving first for Logan is that he would need to stand to let Ivanov get to his seat. This subtle, perfectly mundane feature of ants sorting or animals herding would create an opportunity for Logan to establish an initial polite and jovial connection. Ivanov would learn that his neighbor for the flight was perfectly hygienic, friendly, and conscientious. Logan, in turn, might ascertain the thickness of his accent, the smell or absence of alcohol on his breath, and whether he is or is not an anxious flyer.

Every detail is a data point in the composition of a profile. Every interaction creates a hypothesis, and testing that hypothesis creates questions, and the pursuit of answers to those questions generates a new hypothesis, refining and refining, until Logan can accurately predict what a man dreams about, where in life he feels unfulfilled, what was his relationship with his father, and so on.

As Logan approaches his seat, he is suddenly faced with an unexpected scenario. Of all the time spent ruminating in anticipation over the hundred different directions a conversation with Ivanov might take, he never once considered the possibility that he could arrive at his seat only to find it already occupied. She is a frail woman with dark, graying hair and a bob haircut, although the hairstyle is more of an unkempt accident than anything deliberate. She appears to be approximately sixty-five years old and wears a red sweatshirt and loose-fitting black pants. She is dressed for comfort, not luxury. Sitting hunched over, she doesn't acknowledge Logan as he stops in front of his seat, with the line of passengers boarding behind him stopping to wait.

"Excuse me, ma'am, I think you might be sitting in my seat," says Logan politely.

The frail woman looks up to acknowledge him, and in the process she reveals a sling on one of her arms. She moves her free hand up to her arm in the sling, appearing to wince as she makes eye contact with Logan.

"Oh, yes, I'm sorry," she responds, "but this aisle actually has more room, and I am in so much pain with my arm." She pauses, as if for dramatic effect, and then continues, "It would be really helpful if I could have the extra room to stretch out. I hope you don't mind. The flight attendant said it would be OK."

The line of passengers behind Logan begin to huff and puff and demonstrate their impatience. In any other context, these might be the slowest people in the world, but suddenly, in this moment, they have not a second to spare. Logan must think quickly. He must be assertive but respectful. Being an asshole now will seem too sudden of a change in demeanor, leaving him appearing a bit too desperate to retain this particular seat.

"I'm sorry, ma'am, but I actually would prefer to have my originally assigned seat," Logan responds.

He can feel his heart rate increasing. Be cool, he tells himself. The delay, however, has caught the attention of the flight attendant, a seasoned, stern-looking woman who appears to prefer efficiency over pleasantry. She approaches.

"Hi sir. This woman actually has a very painful injury to her arm. Do you mind if she swaps seats with you?"

Quick to respond, Logan replies, "Actually, I kind of have this personal rule where I don't change seats. It's just a personal thing; I'm sorry."

The flight attendant lets out a loud, disapproving sigh. Her iron fist is clearly not accustomed to pushback. Meanwhile, the nearby passengers close enough to be privy to the situation begin to quietly mutter among themselves, making judgmental frowns toward Logan for not letting the poor injured passenger have her way. The flight attendant turns toward the injured woman reluctantly.

"I'm sorry ma'am. You'll have to go back to your original seat. Some people can be kind of superstitious about their seats, I'm afraid."

Yes, thinks Logan. That's it! Superstition is all.

The poor, poor injured interloper lets out a loud sigh of her own and slowly stands up, but not without the requisite theatrics. Moving into the aisle in slow motion, her loud, exaggerated sounds of painful agony seem designed to maximize the embarrassment for Logan.

"Ahh, it hurts, ohhhhh, owwwwww." She gesticulates audibly, lightly tapping her sling to be sure the world knows what a cruel, cruel man Logan must be. "Excuse me, I'm sorry, I just need to get by you. Ahhh, ohhh…"

She trails off and Logan jumps into his seat, seeking refuge from the scorn. He keeps his head down as the remaining passengers board. The notoriety that has befallen him in such short order makes him feel as if any attempt to maintain a low profile has been eradicated. Amid all of his internal angst, Logan neglects to spot Mikhail Ivanov slowly approaching in line. When he finally arrives in the aisle and motions that he has the inner seat, Logan is practically surprised, as if he forgot a fellow passenger would be occupying the seat next to his. Ironically, this works to Logan's advantage, as he appears anything other than a man anticipating an expected outcome. He glances up and smiles, standing and moving out of the way so that Ivanov can maneuver to his seat. Logan politely says hello in the process.

"Hello. I'm sorry; let me move my bag out of the way here a bit," remarks Logan. Logan motions toward his bag on the ground, shuffling it out of the way from Ivanov's leg room.

"Oh, hello. That's no problem, thank you. I have plenty of room," responds Ivanov.

The response is reciprocal and friendly, spoken with a subtle Russian accent and a soft tone. Now up close, Logan assesses the small details of Ivanov's style. His brown dress shoes are sleek and tidy. They don't appear new, but they do appear to be polished. He wears a very mild cologne with a faint smell of vetiver. As he leans over to set his laptop bag down, the sleeve of his tan blazer shifts upward slightly, revealing a vintage wristwatch with a light brown leather strap and a tan watch face with Cyrillic lettering. Like his shoes, the watch doesn't appear to be expensive, but the pristine presentation suggests a meticulous attention to detail. Logan's immediate impression in this moment is to assume that his own handlers underestimated Ivanov, or at least they had alluded to a less sophisticated man.

As they both settle into their seats, Logan refrains from talking. His goal is to wait for an opportunity later into the flight, hopefully finding a moment that feels organic, without appearing eager or pressured. He pulls out a paperback book with a semi-intriguing title on human consciousness, a potential conversation starter if Ivanov is feeling curious. Ivanov, meanwhile, simply sits and waits for the flight to begin takeoff procedures. No headphones, no book, no devices. He stares out the window, never glancing around the plane at his fellow passengers. Once in the air, as soon as permission is granted, he pulls out his laptop, followed by a pair of headphones. There is no pause convenient enough to allow Logan time to plant the initial seeds of rapport. In the moment, he feels ill-prepared for this entire experience and wonders whether anyone could have pulled off delaying the use of Ivanov's headphones while still appearing natural.

The headphones go in and a Russian film begins playing on Ivanov's laptop. Unfortunately for Logan, this is not a film that he recognizes. Another lost opportunity for connection. This continues, one man on his device and the other in a book, for about an hour, until Ivanov hits pause and removes the headphones, turning to Logan to ask if he would mind moving so that he can walk to the restroom.

"Do you mind if I get through here for a moment? I need to use the restroom." Again, the Russian accent is subtle.

"No, not at all," Logan responds.

"Thank you," answers Ivanov politely with a smile.

Logan stands, allowing him space to step into the aisle. A few minutes pass, allowing Logan time to consider his next move. This may be the only opportunity to engage. The target returns and politely asks to step by once again.

"Pardon me, back again."

"No problem at all."

They go through the motions, but before Ivanov has the opportunity to put his headphones back on, Logan makes his play.

"I hope you don't mind me asking, but is that a Russian accent I think I heard?"

Ivanov smiles politely and responds. "Yes, yes, I am Russian."

Logan responds enthusiastically, "Ah, Ya govor-yu po Rooski, no nee manogo. (I speak Russian, but not much.)"

To his surprise, Ivanov seems genuinely excited.

"You speak Russian! Ochen horosho! (Very nice!)"

"Not quite as well as I would like, I'm afraid," responds Logan with humility.

Ivanov lets out a surprisingly hearty laugh.

"Well, it sounds like perhaps your Russian is better than my English!"

"I don't know about that," responds Logan, with a smile. "I rarely get an opportunity to speak in Russian these days. What brings you to the states?"

A brief alteration in microexpressions sweeps across Ivanov's face. Logan suddenly experiences an internal worry that he moved too fast.

"I live here, actually, in DC," answers Ivanov. "I am from Moscow, but DC is home for now."

"I'm Logan, by the way."

He extends his hand and Ivanov reciprocates. A gentle handshake, but professional, occurring simultaneously with very deliberate eye contact, as if Ivanov had practiced this a hundred times before implementing it a thousand more. In this split second, Logan forms a hypothesis that Ivanov was not born into a world of business deals. He has built success for himself but likely comes from humble origins. There is a warmth to him that puts the mind at ease. An absence of arrogance.

"I'm Mikhail. Ochen pri-yat-no (Nice to meet you)," he responds in kind.

"So how does Washington, DC, compare to Moscow?" asks Logan.

Mikhail chuckles.

"I don't really like it, to be honest. It's too much like a small village. I'd much prefer New York, or maybe Colorado."

"Colorado is great," responds Logan. "Have you been there before?"

Mikhail responds excitedly, "Only to ski once, with my family. I loved it!"

"I enjoy the mountains very much as well, although I'm embarrassed to admit that I look rather foolish on skis," Logan replies.

Mikhail laughs again, seemingly finding Logan's apparent honesty to be an endearing feature.

"So did your family love Colorado as much as you? I'm guessing they're not too fond of Washington, DC, either?" asks Logan.

"Well, my wife, she does not like the city. I have three kids, two sons here. They're young, too young to have ever known

Moscow. My daughter, I think she would love to ski, but she's…not here. She stays in Moscow. Teenager, you know, she has troubles…Are you from Texas? Traveling for work, or fun perhaps?" asks Mikhail, seemingly eager to change the subject.

"I live in DC as well, actually. I'm completing my doctorate there. Unfortunately I am not traveling for fun," replies Logan with a laugh. "I was attending a conference. Nothing particularly exciting I'm afraid."

"A conference on human consciousness, perhaps?" inquires Mikhail, with a slightly mischievous smile as he points at Logan's paperback book.

Logan laughs again. "You are not far off, actually! I'm working on my doctorate in clinical psychology, and we have to go to these conferences sometimes. This was a group relations conference."

Mikhail is only more curious now and digs deeper. "What is this 'group relations'?"

"It's basically," responds Logan, "an opportunity for academics to get together and feel bad about themselves while they pay too much money for overeducated facilitators to point out their shortcomings."

Logan's improvised attempt at a joke is meant to serve the dual purpose of also shutting down any additional questions about the nonexistent conference that he was told he would not need to discuss. The joke, awkwardly, contains too much American nuance for Mikhail Ivanov to react accordingly.

"So, with clinical psychology, this means that you help people with their mental problems?" asks Mikhail.

"I certainly try," answers Logan. "I also do some really interesting research, or at least I think it's really interesting, on terrorism and extremist violence. You know, looking at, or trying to understand, why or how people turn to violence."

"Ochen eenteresno! (Very interesting)," responds Mikhail. He continues, "Also sounds very complicated. You do good things for the world. You will make an excellent psychologist."

"Thank you for saying that," responds a sincere Logan.

Suddenly the plane's intercom cuts into the conversation to announce the approach for landing. The conversation had been remarkably pleasant, thinks Logan, to the point that he nearly forgot his objective. He reaches into his pocket and grabs a business card.

"Well, it was very nice chatting with you. If you ever want to grab a drink sometime, feel free to give me a call," remarks Logan, as he hands Mikhail his card. "I hope you make it back to Colorado someday."

Mikhail responds warmly. "Very nice to meet you as well! Spasiba Bolshoi! (Thank you!)."

The exit from the plane is smooth and without issue, but Logan's subsequent walk through Reagan National Airport feels strangely isolating and surreal. Was this mission a success? It felt as though a tremendous amount of effort had gone into arranging a singular conversation, albeit a rather friendly one. Perhaps this is the key Logan needs to remember. Friendly. The conversation had been rather friendly. Information gathering had felt secondary to relationship building, but both in hindsight seem like relative successes.

Exiting the airport, Logan immediately hails a cab and gives the driver the address for his rendezvous point with Brock.

"3323 Tulman, in Bethesda, please. The Irish Tavern."

"Irish Tavern. You got it."

The cab takes off down the road and Logan calls his handler. The call is brief, lapidarian, free of affirmation.

"I'm en route to rendezvous point. ETA one five mike," speaks Logan into the phone. The unnecessarily strict military parlance was uttered partially in jest, meant to curb his own insecurity.

"Good. Hope it was a successful trip," responds Brock on the other end of the line. "Go ahead and turn your phone off now. Keep it off. I'll see you soon."

Logan turns his phone off and relaxes, letting the tension exit from his body if only for a moment, exhaling for what feels like the first time in days. The cab driver is quiet and Logan welcomes the silence. Traffic flows at an acceptable pace. Over the Potomac, past the Lincoln Memorial, cutting through Rock Creek Park. Logan watches the trees, the greenery in the midst of a treacherous town. The sunlight dances across his face. He feels cautiously optimistic, wondering if, perhaps, he made someone somewhere proud today.

The Irish Tavern eventually emerges into view. The restaurant is built like a Tudor-style home, a combination of cream-colored walls with dark wood and stone masonry. Brock stands outside the entrance, waiting. His attire is casual, with jeans and a button-up shirt with the sleeves slightly rolled up. He wears aviator sunglasses. His beard appears thicker and less well groomed. In spite of his best efforts, he looks like a mercenary, or an FBI agent trying too hard to blend in. He watches as Logan's cab pulls up, but he remains still, observing, watching to be certain Logan steps out alone, watching to be certain the cab wasn't followed.

Logan steps out calmly, giving Brock a nod that all is well. Unlike their prior debriefs with cavalier attitudes and underwhelming dive bars, Logan immediately senses a level of seriousness in Brock that suggests this meeting is nothing trivial. No words are exchanged between the two men yet, as Brock turns and opens the door to the restaurant, holding it open for Logan.

The interior is fairly crowded for midday, and Logan can feel that tension start to return to his body. The lighting is dim throughout, casting shadows on the Tudor aesthetic. A long mahogany-wood bar nearly stretches across the full length of one side of the restaurant. Behind the bar, hundreds of different types of whiskey and bourbon line the wall. As Logan and Brock walk to a table reserved in the far corner of the restaurant, Logan scans the crowd of patrons. Mostly over forty, many far older. Financially secure, but not pretentious. This is clearly a favored local choice for those who can afford living nearby. His gaze fixes upon a man standing alone at the bar who seems out of place in comparison. The man's face is covered with a well-groomed, closely cropped dark beard. Built like Brock, with a muscular frame, he's dressed casually in a light green athletic jacket with the sleeves pulled up slightly, revealing a thick black military-style watch on one wrist. So often their watches give them away, considers Logan silently, adding a bit of levity to his thoughts. This lone drinker doesn't budge as Logan and Brock pass by, finding their seat at a small table in the back.

Finally, Brock speaks. "Welcome to the Irish Tavern. Ever been here before?"

"No, first time. Nice place. I trust you're not alone,"responds Logan.

"Huh?" asks Brock, failing to appear genuinely naïve.

"Dude at the bar, my ten o'clock," Logan answers. "Also, this place is a bit crowded, isn't it?"

"We can never be too careful in these situations. Don't worry about the crowd. It's all about hiding in plain sight. Anyway, well? Let's hear it."

Before Logan can begin, the waitress arrives and quickly ascertains that this is a table that prefers her presence be minimal. Logan orders a stout, Brock a water, and she scurries off.

"Well for starters, he's a family man. Two young sons and a wife here in the states who live with him in DC. Guessing you already knew that. The wife is not crazy about the city. Neither is Ivanov. Here's something you may not know about his family: He's also got a teenage daughter back in Moscow. Seems like she's some kind of troublemaker. Or she's in trouble. It was a bit hazy, but the word "trouble" was definitely used in referring to her."

"Hazy, as in you don't remember the details?" interjects Brock. "Or hazy as in he was sparse with the details?"

"Definitely the latter. I could see on his face that there was some kind of emotional turmoil there. Whatever the issue with the teenager, I got the sense that's why she stayed behind."

"So he told you he doesn't like DC? Tell me more about that."

"Right. Describes it as a small village. Didn't mean that from a positive lens. Says he would much prefer New York or Colorado, with a heavy emphasis on Colorado. You could tell Mikhail was kind of mesmerized with skiing and the mountains."

Logan has a gentle half smile on his face when he makes this last point, hinting at a touch of endearment for his new-found Russian friend. Brock notices.

"Mikhail, huh? First-name basis? How did you feel about the guy? What was the mood, what was the vibe when you made your approach?" asks Brock.

"I liked him. He has a certain charm, a certain charisma. The language barrier was not too intense. Felt like the rapport building started from the get-go. Of course, I'm acutely aware that you guys could share with me that he's actually some diabolical, evil motherfucker, but in that space, he seemed to genuinely appreciate the connection."

"Hmm, doesn't sound like a bad start to me," replies Brock. "This is good stuff. Really good. You hungry? You should try their prime rib. The best in town. On me."

Logan wonders where they might meet if any of the costs incurred were actually subtracted directly from the pockets of his handler. Brock makes eye contact with the waitress as she grabs Logan's beer off the bar and brings it over. Both men order the prime rib. A delicious meal on Uncle Sam's dime. Logan needs the sustenance almost as much as he needs sleep. The dark circles under his eyes are set so deeply that he fears he might start drawing unwanted attention from worried old ladies. As desperate as he is for a respite, there is more intel to convey. And he needs to get paid.

Logan and Brock would spend the next hour and a half discussing, in painstaking detail, every aspect of the completed operation. They did so in between bites of a fairly decent prime rib. Logan shares details about Ivanov's laptop—"Expensive but built for media or gaming." He mentions the film Ivanov was watching—"Russian, probably late 90s, something to do with mobsters." Logan discusses the lady in red, with the sling, to which Brock replies, "Oh this will definitely become a training scenario." Meanwhile, the onlooker never comes around. He orders his own plate of food and drinks his own pints. There is a mirror across from him at the bar. Occasionally he will glance over, but never anything too obvious. Logan assumes this is protocol, but he also can't help but wonder what the worst-case scenario might be that would cause the man at the bar to spring into action. Finally, their bellies full and Logan's details drained, the moment arrives for the cash.

"Well, I guess it's about that time," remarks Brock. "Go ahead and reach under the table. I've got your money in the envelope. Five grand. Like we agreed."

Logan reaches under and grabs the envelope, quickly placing it in the pocket of his blazer. Suddenly it occurs to him that he never once asked about the risk, about lingering threats, about Russian intelligence services being acutely aware of his identity.

"So, is there any danger for me now?" asks Logan. "Assuming he reports his encounter with me to his people, what will they do?

"There are certainly no guarantees, but you're fine. Sounds like you were a natural. Maybe our guy didn't think it was even necessary to raise the issue with his security officer. But, if they do look into you, the good news is that you are exactly who you said you are. You might start getting a lot of spam in your email, maybe weird messages, phishing stuff. Just ignore it all. But otherwise, nothing to be worried about. Remember though, if Ivanov emails, texts, calls, whatever, you let me know immediately."

CHAPTER 10

A full week passes before another round of excitement. A quiet week. Intense, slow. Intense, slow. The hurry up and wait is such a feature of life in the military that it has become a universally accepted maxim among all members. But now, away from all that, Logan exists in some strange purgatory between lost civilian and the red right hand of a city upon a hill. So he waits instead of living. The silence is not rejuvenating, but maddening. And then one day, he gets an email.

Jogging on a path in a wooded park in Arlington, he is drenched in sweat, running hard, focused. Sporting dark running shorts, a short-sleeve T-shirt, a backward black baseball cap, and headphones in his ears, he punishes himself with the distance until he glances at his phone when a new email arrives. Logan freezes in his tracks. Mikhail Ivanov has made contact. He ponders his next move, steps off the running path, and immediately calls Brock.

"Hey man, guess who just emailed me?"

"No shit?" replies Brock. "What'd he say?"

"Very cordial. Said he appreciated our 'vibrant in-air discussion.' He wants to meet up for a glass of wine tomorrow night. Said he finds 'psychology and the human mind fascinating.' I can't do it tomorrow though. The girl I started seeing, my classmate, I'm supposed to meet her parents for the first time tomorrow night. I can find a different date for Ivanov."

"Well, did you respond to him yet? Let's think about this. Don't rule it out. I don't need to remind you how important this is for the Bureau."

"I hear you, man, but this relationship with her is important to me too. I don't want to fuck it up. And you guys should want me in a good headspace anyway, right? Let me figure out my calendar, find some options for Mikhail, and I'll facilitate something. Will keep you in the loop."

Later that afternoon, in a nearby coffee shop, Christie joins Logan for a productive few hours of graduate school work. New Orleans jazz music lightly plays over a speaker, a particular theme at this establishment. Seated across from each other at a small round table, their laptops are open and the studious environment is only occasionally disrupted by the sound of a bell on the door that jingles with the arrival of each new customer. Logan makes brief eye contact with Christie, peering at her over the edge of their laptops. She can tell he is both ruminating and working hard to refrain from speaking.

"What is it? What's going on in that beautiful brain of yours?" she asks.

"I was just thinking about tomorrow. Seven p.m., right?"

Christie lets out a sigh and appears mildly annoyed.

"That's the third time you've asked me that today. Yes, seven p.m.! Somebody must be a little nervous to meet the parents."

Logan laughs, knowing that she's right. He is nervous. Nervous about letting Brock down, and yes, nervous about meeting her parents.

"Alright, yeah, fair enough. I just want to make a good impression," replies Logan.

"Nobody makes a good impression with my parents," she responds.

"Well, that's comforting."

Christie laughs audibly before making a cute gesture to cover her mouth, as if they are in a library and not a business with distant trombones and jingling doors. The moment is cute and Logan wishes he could bottle it up, save her church-girl innocence for a dreary day, whenever a "break glass in the event of nihilism" experience arises. They both return to their work, but only briefly. A few minutes later, Christie's expression suddenly changes. A perplexed frown splashes across her face.

"What's wrong?" asks Logan.

"I don't...know...I just got this weird email."

"What do you mean? Like junk mail?"

The moment feels tense, no longer playful. Christie's eyes move slowly from her laptop up to Logan. She stares at him. The silence lasts for five years until she breaks it with a question.

"Do you remember that night we were supposed to study together for the midterm? When you showed up late, and drunk?"

"Yeah, look," he responds, "I won't fuck this up tomorrow night, I promise. I don't know if they'll like me, but I want to—"

She cuts him off. "What did you do that night after I left? You told me you felt really bad. That you fell asleep thinking about how you were going to make it up to me."

"Uh yeah, haven't we already talked about this?" asks a confused Logan. "What's the problem?"

In one quick motion, Christie abruptly turns her laptop around to face Logan, revealing a video playing on her laptop screen. She points at the screen and yells, "Well then who the fuck is that!?"

Logan stares at the screen in shock. With remarkable clarity, a video displays him having sex with Katya, taken from inside of his apartment. He struggles to find words.

"Oh my God. Christie, I am so sorry. I was really drunk that night. I did feel really bad—"

She interrupts again, "Yeah it looks like you're feeling realllly bad in this video! Fuck it. I can't believe I actually thought this would work."

Christie rises from the table and slams her laptop shut. As she stands, the motion of her body shakes the table, spilling their coffee. She grabs her bag off the ground and storms out, trying to avoid sobbing loudly as she goes. She is unsuccessful. Logan, meanwhile, remains seated in a state of disbelief. An awkward silence permeates throughout the coffee shop now as the other customers look on, seemingly in secondhand embarrassment. What is a compromised identity when you're merely playing the role of yourself, wonders Logan. With haste, Logan packs up his belongings, desperate to escape the whispers and prying eyes. It all feels more real now that it is personal.

Logan quickly walks to the nearby Arlington metro station, calling Brock along the way. His mood is angry, his judgment clouded. He is paranoid but lacking in discretion. He possesses a deficit of discipline to recognize when the desire for retribution could interfere with the need to be tactical. Pausing on the stairwell to the metro station, he yells into the phone.

"So how the fuck did they get a camera into my fucking apartment!? Shouldn't you guys be looking out for shit like this?"

Brock, on the other end of the line and seemingly unfazed, responds, "Listen, man, if you had told us about hooking up with Katya from the beginning then we probably could have kept our eyes open for something like this. It was obviously the Russians, but this was probably some small-time criminal shit. Maybe Katya thought you were rich and wanted to blackmail you but changed her mind when she realized you're just a student. Maybe she told the boyfriend you beat up about the video later on. Maybe he was in on it from the beginning. I'm sorry, man. We'll look into it. It's definitely not the kind of thing that a high-level dude like Ivanov would know anything about, so you'd still be safe meeting with him. Anyway, I'm sure you've had enough of dealing with the Russians after today, so no worries if you want to back off. You can give all the Ivanov shit a break. We get it."

"No, fuck that," replies Logan. "It's on now, man. I'm setting up the meeting with Ivanov for tomorrow. They're going to come into my house and watch me? No. I want these bastards to hurt."

* * *

Sitting alone at an upscale cocktail bar in DC, Logan waits for his target to arrive. He prefers cocktails, sure, but this establishment teeters on the edge of pretension. The ice cubes are large single squares. Everything is infused with this or that. There is too much mezcal and too many lobbyists on the prowl. But this is Ivanov's preferred location. While he waits for him to walk through the front entrance, Logan notices that his hand is starting to shake. He finds the adrenaline a bit humorous. For someone haunted by images of confirmed kills, as a morally injured hunter of man, here he is shaking in anticipation of an interpersonal chess match. Stop it, he tells himself. His hand is still.

Mikhail Ivanov walks through the entrance and searches for Logan. Business casual. Blazer. Slacks. Relaxed but formal. His posture and movements are slightly awkward, youthful almost, like a socially anxious adolescent teenager attending his first party. His affable nature could prove disarming. Logan stands and waves him over to the table. They smile and shake hands like old friends.

"Ah, Logan, how are you? It's good to see you."

Logan responds, "Great to see you, Mikhail. I appreciate the invitation. It's always good to make new friends in DC."

His watch is different this time, observes Logan. A Rolex. While not much of a watch man himself, naïveté is no hindrance to recognizing such expense. While not glaringly flashy, it seems out of character for Ivanov. More data for Logan.

The two men sit down and quickly glance at the cocktail menu. The list is short but perhaps more complex than it ought to be. Mikhail seems to acknowledge this.

"Logan, what do you think? Do you like this place?"

"Da (Yes). I have never been here before, but the drinks look good. Ochen een-ter-esnie (Very interesting)," responds Logan.

"Horosho! (Good!)" replies Mikhail. "I have never been here either but I thought you would perhaps appreciate this place. You are a man of refined tastes, no?"

"Thank you, Mikhail," responds Logan with a slight laugh and appreciation for the compliment, the receipt of which was never a particularly strong suit for him.

"I read your paper recently, on the psychology of lone wolf terrorism," remarks Mikhail. "Very impressive."

"Oh, thank you. I'm glad someone read it!"

Logan's attempt at humor to diffuse his discomfort with positive praise does not appear to resonate with Mikhail.

"No, really, very interesting," continues Mikhail. "This is real problem in Russia too, you know. The, how did you say it, radicalization process?"

"Yes, of course. I'm a bit familiar with the issue of Chechen extremists—"

Mikhail interjects, "Well not just Chechen. It's a very big problem. Have you ever thought about writing a paper in Russian?"

"It never occurred to me," Logan responds. "But I wouldn't be opposed to it. Maybe we could write a paper together?"

"No, no. It's not my area. Eta my-yo leech-no-ye muh-nen-i-yuh. (This is just my personal opinion)."

"Da, ya poni-my-yoo. (I understand)," responds Logan.

Mikhail's demeanor shifts slightly into something more serious.

"Many of us have lost family members to terrorist attacks, you see?" adds Mikhail.

"Have you," Logan pauses mid-question, as if the delicacy only hits him after he begins to speak, and then starts again, "Have you…lost a family member?"

Mikhail sits momentarily in quiet reflection. He looks away as sadness sweeps across his face, eliciting an apology from Logan.

"I'm sorry, Mikhail. That was rude of me. I shouldn't ask such things."

"My daughter," responds Mikhail, without looking directly at Logan. "She was killed in Moscow in 1999, in apartment bombing. She was only sixteen. My beautiful Anechka."

His eyes begin to well up with tears, but he is too careful to let them fall.

"I'm so sorry, Mikhail," Logan responds. "I remember those bombings."

Mikhail's gaze returns to Logan. A tinge of anger is present but never directed at the man sitting across from him. Rather, some distant foe bears responsibility for this heartache.

"Yes, so you see, it is not just the Chechens who are the extremists…In any case, we are here for drinks and good conversation. I do not mean to discuss such seriousness. But I think you do good work. Tell me, Logan, why did you become a psychologist? Is it because you make people feel comfortable to talk about their pain? You must like to help people, no?"

"Almost a psychologist," Logan interjects. "I still need to finish my remaining coursework and complete my doctoral internship. But I don't want to bore you with those details. You're right; I do like to help people. It is certainly preferable to—

A waitress arrives at their table before Logan can continue, leaving both men to realize that they've been chatting as if they're old colleagues reuniting after a long absence, and the setting had mattered very little, until the point that the waitress with the slender legs and staid expression arrived to remind them that they were in a drinking establishment. In a moment of haste, Logan orders the cocktail with egg white, and rye, and honey. He hopes the rye is not an afterthought. Mikhail in turn points to the menu at something with vanilla bean and half a dozen liqueurs that neither men can pronounce with any certainty.

The making of the drinks behind the bar is itself a spectacle, and Mikhail seems particularly entertained by this. Another of his endearing qualities. The conversation between the two men lasts for just over two hours, with each choosing to imbibe two cocktails, although Logan is strongly considering ordering a third. For once it didn't feel necessary. The smoothness of the conversation and his ability to abstain felt foreign as a pairing, to the point of perplexity. Logan seemed to genuinely *enjoy* the conversation. Outside of the bar, the two men eventually say their goodbyes, with a warm handshake and warmer words.

"Thank you for this, Mikhail. It was nice to have such a meaningful conversation."

"Yes, very nice," Mikhail responds. "Let's meet again soon. Logan I think you should meet my family. My wife, she makes excellent pirozhki. Loo-beet-yuh peeroshki? (Do you like pirozhki?)"

"Very much so, Mikhail. And I would be honored to meet them."

"Well then, it's settled. Perhaps next week?"

They part ways, with both men hailing separate cabs that drive off in different directions.

Logan is excited to arrange the debrief with Brock afterwards, nearly forgetting about his anger with the Christie situation, about his frustration toward his handlers for not adequately having his back. He is a golden retriever returning with a stick and hoping his owner will be proud of the dog he has become. When he calls Brock to discuss the next steps, Harry answers instead.

"Oh," says Logan into the phone. "I was just trying to reach Brock to set up our debrief. A lot of good stuff to review."

"No debrief this time," replies Harry. "Brock is on a training assignment out West. He'll be back soon. In the meantime, stay the course. Good work."

The call feels anticlimactic and bittersweet. Sure, he received a mild pat on the head, but Harry's lack of enthusiasm leaves him feeling like a kid excited on Christmas morning only to discover that all his presents under the tree contain sweatpants. Logan will stay the course, as directed, but he'll still be craving some kind of Christmas magic and hoping Grandma's house has the real gifts yet to come.

The next invitation from Mikhail would arrive four days later, again via email:

> Logan,
>
> Please join us for dinner on Saturday. We will be honored to have you as our guest. My wife will make her famous pirozhki. We will have wine. Will 7:00 PM be good? Our address is located at 2104 Vermont.
>
> Your friend,
> Mikhail

* * *

The small brownstone stands on a relatively quiet and nondescript street. There is nothing to suggest this particular neighborhood is salient with Russians or other Eastern Europeans. The requisite homeless population wanders the sidewalks two blocks down. Logan once made the assumption that Mikhail Ivanov lived within the Russian Embassy compound or at least within property owned by the Russian government. This, from Logan's perspective on the exterior, appears to be nothing more than an average DC townhouse. Sunset is nearing as Logan walks up the short set of stairs and knocks. He is nervous, less about being in the home of a potential foreign agent and more due to concerns about how far his conversational Russian speaking abilities can take him in a family setting. One-on-one interactions are quite different from wives and children, who might possibly be less forgiving of poor conjugation. Behind the door, Logan can hear footsteps and the yelling of small boys.

Mikhail opens the front door, greeting Logan with a smile and a handshake. He holds a bottle of wine in one hand, as if he had just been preparing a pour when the knock arrived. Standing approximately five feet behind Mikhail is a slightly mousy brunette woman with mildly graying hair and wire-framed glasses. While not immediately conventionally attractive, she has the look of a tired Soviet librarian. The standard deviation of her age might have been plus or minus a full decade. She is short and wears a light-colored dress with a fading floral pattern. Mikhail is quick with the introduction.

"Etto moyah szhena, Paulina. (This is my wife, Paulina.)"

Logan steps forward to shake her hand. "Menyah zo-voot Logan. Ochen pri-yat-no, Paulina. (My name is Logan. Very nice to meet you, Paulina."

Paulina reciprocates the handshake, but opts for English. "Very nice to meet you as well, Logan. It is our pleasure to have you for dinner." Her Russian accent is present but less pronounced than Mikhail's.

"Doctor Logan!" shouts Mikhail, with a smile.

"Not quite yet!" responds Logan, laughing and slightly embarrassed.

Standing behind Paulina are two young boys in matching blue shirts with matching bow ties. They appear rather shy and quite skeptical of the American houseguest.

"These young men are my sons, Leo and Alexander," states Mikhail, pointing to the youngsters hiding behind their mother. "Boys, say hello to our guest, Mr. Logan," he requests firmly.

The two boys, ages eight and ten, step forward and shake Logan's hand, one at a time. Adorned with their red bow ties, they treat the occasion with such formality that Logan must consciously resist the urge to chuckle.

"Hello, Mr. Logan. I am Alexander," states the older boy. He steps back after the handshake and makes room for his younger brother to step forward.

"Hello Mr. Logan. I am Leo."

Both boys speak in such perfect English that Logan, for a fleeting moment, imagines them in Moscow, struggling to assimilate, torn between two worlds, a childhood in the West and ancestry in the East.

Logan looks at Mikhail and nods. "Such intelligent and respectable boys, Mikhail. Leo, the young Tolstoy, and Alexander, the young Pushkin," he says with a smile.

"Solzhenitsyn," responds Mikhail, laughing.

"Logan, please come and sit down and enjoy some wine," says Paulina, perhaps growing impatient with the conversation in the foyer. "Dinner will be ready soon."

Mikhail invites Logan to follow him into the dining room, showing him to his seat at the table. As Logan sits, Mikhail pours glasses of red wine for the two of them, before sitting down at the end of the table next to Logan. The young boys move elsewhere into the home to do young boy things while Paulina scurries off into the kitchen.

"I hope Khvanchkara is to your liking," remarks Mikhail, raising his wine glass. "It is from Georgia. Not too sweet, but sweet enough."

Logan raises his glass and responds, "Za nashe zdorovya! (To our health!)."

Periodically throughout the evening an ounce of reality drifts into Logan's consciousness, reminding him where he is and why he is here. His relationship with Mikhail feels strangely genuine though. Spy bonding with spy from a place of mutual respect. Ivanov's family is real, as is his home. Within the walls of this brownstone, within the courtesies of Mikhail Ivanov's benevolence, Logan finds admiration, rather than some anticipated Potemkin village. There is a growing level of cognitive dissonance within him, and Logan has not yet fully discovered how to use his own empathy as an advantage.

Eventually, Paulina brings out the food. Traditional Russian dishes, but she seems none too pleased about any of it. She then darts off to round up the boys, still polite and well-behaved as they take their seats. The spread is rather vast. There is a soup with pickled cucumbers, cold fish, a potato salad on the side, and, of course, the famous pirozhki. In contrast with all other elements of the evening, the meal itself feels the most performative. Logan suspects the family does not normally eat like this, but Mikhail is closely watching his every reaction to the tastes, sights, and smells. Paulina struggles to crack an honest smile throughout. She is kind, but some state of tension seems to exist between her and Mikhail. Logan hopes he is not the cause of it.

After about thirty minutes, in a very matter-of-fact fashion, Paulina suddenly asks, "Well, Mr. Logan, you seem to speak our native language very well. May I ask, where did you learn Russian?"

Mikhail appears embarrassed, interpreting her antics as overly forward. He attempts to address this. "Paulina, pochemu (why)—"

"What? I would like to know," she responds abruptly, cutting him off.

For the first time, it occurs to Logan how peculiar it is that he has not yet been asked this question. He knew the moment would eventually arrive, but he was still caught off guard when it finally did. He is playing himself in this role, though, and there is little utility in obfuscation. So he tells the truth.

"I studied Russian in a military institute, in California. I'm a bit embarrassed though, because I rarely have the opportunity to practice it. I went off to a couple of wars instead. And now, I suppose I jump at the opportunity to engage with Russian speakers, in spite of my, perhaps, poor speaking and comprehension."

He hopes his humility will stifle follow-up questions, but instead of affirmations and redirections, the youngest of the boys, Leo, asks a blunt question of his own.

"Mr. Logan, did you ever kill anybody in war?"

Mikhail grows angry quickly and yells at the boy. "Leo! That is not polite! Apologize to our guest immediately!"

"I'm sorry, Mr. Logan," responds Leo.

The boy is straight-faced but seemingly confused by his father's reaction. Logan feels bad for the kid. He never makes a big deal about such questions, but he wouldn't fault a child for a failure in conscientiousness anyway. Before Logan can conjure up an appropriate reply to match the sentiment, the older of the two boys joins in the conversation.

"Our father fought in war in Afghanistan," says the young Alexander.

"Father, did you ever kill anyone in Afghanistan?" asks Leo, in a moment of nearly comedic perseveration.

The look of utter astonishment on Mikhail's face is so profound that Logan must consciously fight the urge to roll off his chair in laughter right then and there. Unfortunately for the boy, his father is not amused.

"Sloo-shy-tye menya! Nyet! Nay govoreet-yeh gloo-postee! (Listen to me! No! Don't talk nonsense!)" shouts Mikhail. "Now go away!"

Tears begin to well up in the boy's eyes as he stands quickly, grabs his plate of half-eaten food, and walks off into the kitchen, defeated. His brother, Alexander, follows next, carrying his own plate away. Paulina, meanwhile, shoots her husband a scornful look before rising from the table. Her gaze meets Logan's and she nods.

"Mr. Logan, thank you for joining us."

Logan stands and responds, "Thank you for having me. It was my honor. The food was amazing."

He returns to his seat as she disappears into the kitchen, leaving Logan and Mikhail alone once again. There is a brief silence between them. Mikhail stares into his wine glass, pondering, while Logan senses that whatever words come next will be worth the wait. Finally, the silence ends.

"I was nineteen years old," says Mikhail. "Western media called them freedom fighters, but what was this freedom? Mujahideen? Most were not from there. It was like distant planet, and we were kids hunting ghosts in caves, slaughtered in mountains, for what? Communism? Perestroika? Democracy? Men with too many ideas send boys to fight their wars. 'If no one fought except on his own conviction—'"

"'There would be no wars,'" adds Logan, finishing the Tolstoy quote.

Mikhail stands and walks to a nearby liquor cabinet, pulling out a bottle of vodka and two shot glasses. He pours two shots and slides one over to Logan. Raising his shot glass and forming a somewhat defeated smile, he utters, "To new friends."

Logan responds, "To the graveyard of empires."

CHAPTER 11

The culture of gastronomy in DC has begun to evolve with such rapidity that celebrity chefs are equally likely to garner local headlines as were political scandals or beltway miscreants. In contrast, the perpetual multitude of local shootings is rarely front-page news. Nevertheless, Logan's dwindling bank account and rising student loans mean that he can't afford expensive tastes in such an expensive town. So occasionally, he hops on the metro and rides a few stops into Silver Spring, Maryland, where his favorite dive bar sells what he considers to be the best cheap burger around. Logan is somewhat protective of this establishment. He won't bring a date, a friend, or a colleague here. Not out of embarrassment, but rather, he enjoys having a place in the city where he assumes he never has to worry about being seen. By most standards, this is grungy. His feet stick to the floor as he walks. The bar reeks of popcorn and stale beer. Rats roam the exterior.

Logan's dinner with Mikhail Ivanov and his family had occurred only five days prior, but the days since have felt like another lifetime. The assignment is to get close to the target, but the target in this case is a family man with interests not unlike his own. He is learning, by himself, how to hone a tradecraft in compartmentalizing. He can be a saint in one box and a sinner in the other. A mild-mannered new friend one invites over for dinner, and a vessel for catastrophically ransacking through the comforts of one's livelihood. He loathes himself for getting too comfortable in such a role, and thus, he tries hard not to think about it, which means it is invariably on his mind. He wonders about the ratio of psychopaths to neurotics in the world of clandestine affairs. He orders another beer.

The establishment is mostly empty, and Logan's eyes are fixed on the TV above the bar as he drinks the stout placed in front of him. A half-eaten burger and fries rest on his plate. Cable news is running through prosaic stories about weather patterns and oil costs. Logan watches mindlessly until suddenly, the story changes. The normal broadcast stops abruptly to make room for breaking news, catching Logan's attention. The news anchor, purveyor of both mundanity and shock, opts for something shocking on this day. She reports:

"Sorry to interrupt your regularly scheduled programming, folks, but we have a breaking news story. We have just learned that the deceased body of a Russian diplomat has been discovered in a hotel room in the Dupont Circle neighborhood of Washington, DC. We can report few details at this time, but we do know that the body of Mikhail Ivanov, a reported cyber defense expert for the Russian Embassy, has been discovered in his hotel room at the five-star Dupont Cove Inn.

His death appears to be the result of blunt force trauma to the head. Foul play is most certainly suspected in this case. A spokeswoman for the DC Police Department has stated that Russian authorities are cooperating on the investigation, and the FBI is assisting as well. Again, we have few details, but police are releasing video footage of a person of interest in this case. We're throwing that video up on the screen now."

The video appearing on screen, surreptitiously recorded in slightly grainy black-and-white footage without audio, shows Logan sitting with Mikhail Ivanov at the cocktail bar. Their friendly banter appears ominous in the absence of sound or color. The news anchor continues:

"We do not yet have a name for this person of interest, but we do know he arrived in Washington, DC, on a flight out of Texas with Mikhail Ivanov, the deceased diplomat, approximately three weeks ago. He can be seen in this footage meeting with the deceased victim at a, what we're told is a cocktail lounge, in DC. We're also hearing additional reporting, although we are waiting to confirm, that there is possibly some additional footage of this person of interest recently entering the home of the deceased. Police are asking for anyone with information on this man's whereabouts, or any other information related to this case, to please give them a call at the number below."

A phone number for the Washington, DC, police tip line flashes on the bottom of the screen as she continues:

"Again, folks, this is breaking news. A Russian diplomat found dead under what appears to be violent circumstances in a Washington, DC, hotel room. For more details now, let's turn live to Elizabeth Brookman, who is currently outside the Dupont Cove Inn in the Dupont Circle neighborhood of Washington, DC. Elizabeth, are you there…"

Her voice trails off as Logan's stunned mind begins to float through a subterranean tunnel of fading light into an underworld of dissociative drift. Some part of him dies in that moment, becoming a project for a future paleontologist of calcified souls. He might be frozen for seconds, minutes, or hours, but it takes the sound of a dropped spoon from a table in the back to force him to blink. He looks away from the TV and stares into his glass of beer in front of him, remaining motionless. For a fleeting moment, he wonders if he should stand and run, but to where? He knows that his exit from the bar will need to draw as little attention as possible. He knows that perhaps every moment for the rest of his life will need to draw as little attention as possible.

The bartender approaches and asks if he'd like another beer, snapping Logan back to reality. His heart is racing, adrenaline climbing. There's that tremble in his hand again. Pull it together, he thinks to himself. Be cool.

"Can I just get the check, please?" Logan asks.

"Sure thing. How was the burger?" asks the bartender.

"Great as always."

The bartender brings the check and Logan pays immediately. He stands from his seat at the bar and makes his way casually to the exit. He emerges into a crisp night air that feels more silent than it ought to be, as if transported to an old Western film just prior to the ambush. The fluorescent city lights hum as moths flutter about, and somewhere in the distance, a city bus squeals. Traffic on the road in front of the bar is otherwise minimal, and foot traffic is even less robust.

There is no one hopping out of unmarked vans to tackle him to the pavement. Local PD are not waiting for him in a slow-motion dragnet. Gunslingers do not peer over rooftops with revolvers in hand. Logan quickly but calmly scans his surroundings for any indication that he is under surveillance. If they're out there, he doesn't see them, which at the very least reduces the probability that law enforcement is tracking him. No indications of aerial ISR and no nearby pedestrians pretending not to look at him. He reaches into his pocket, pulls out his phone, and turns it off. Facial recognition remains as a lingering concern. Thus, he has to rule out public transportation. But where will he go?

He doesn't have a go bag with him, and he knows that any local contacts will be far too predictable. Logan is unwilling to risk putting the people he cares about in a dangerous situation. Besides, he trusts not a soul, in good times or bad. The news reporter referred to him as a "person of interest," rather than a "suspect." Logan's name is easily identifiable from his airline ticket, and yet that information has not yet been shared with media. Given the absence of patrol cars, a BOLO seems unlikely. Somebody is either protecting Logan or manipulating him, perhaps a combination of the two. He feels entirely ill-prepared for this moment, and he hates to acknowledge that the best option is an absolutely terrible one. He has to go home.

His apartment is approximately four miles away from his current location as the crow flies. He could run there, but he isn't wearing jogging clothes, and this would draw suspicion. He is wearing boots and jeans, not exactly the sartorial choices of a well-adjusted runner training for his next big race. He cannot take the most direct route, as the bustling city sidewalks closer to his apartment would mean risking phone calls to the tip line from onlookers feeling heroic. He has to opt for side roads and the occasional winding path through quiet neighborhoods. He estimates it will take him ninety minutes to traverse this route. Ninety minutes of tension.

He walks at a brisk pace. His eyes and ears latch on to every sound and movement. A breeze lightly blowing through the flowers on well-manicured front lawns. The sound of a car stopping at a stop sign two blocks down. A dog barking in the distance. Logan attempts to avoid looking paranoid, with considerable, counterproductive effort. He grips the knife in his pocket as he walks, ready for whatever comes his way. If local law enforcement finds him, he has no reason to believe the truth would set him free. He is a lone actor; it's doubtful there was ever a paper trail of his work with the FBI. Brock and company can easily maintain plausible deniability, especially if their careers, or lives in general, are on the line in relation to a dead foreign diplomat. If the Russians find him, his fate will perhaps be far worse. Assuming Ivanov's death was ordered by Russian intelligence services, which, logically, is Logan's leading theory, then Logan's perceived public culpability is their perfect alibi. Facilitating the permanent disappearance of Logan would be rather convenient for them. In this case, Logan has little interest in helping them clean house.

As he walks down the sidewalk of a particularly exposed section of his long path to shelter, Logan becomes acutely aware of a car turning the corner that he had passed by moments before. The car pulls up behind him as he walks, trailing him slowly about a hundred feet behind. It could merely be a food delivery for a nearby residence, he thinks to himself, or it could mean a staged robbery and his imminent death. He is the prey with his back turned to the predator. The illuminated Logan glows against the spotlight of the car's headlights, and there is nothing he can do to seek camouflage while remaining on this route. He chooses to stray from his path, turning a corner around a house on the right, another side street. For a brief moment he is out of sight of the potential predator, and he doesn't hesitate, suddenly sprinting with all of his speed, putting as much distance between himself and the car as possible. He quickly turns left around another corner, onto another side street. He slows his pace, acts casual, listens for the sounds, and hears only silence. The rest of the walk is quiet, smooth, and bloodless.

As he nears his apartment complex, Logan slows and takes in the surroundings at about seventy-five yards from the front door. Quiet, eerily so, but stopping now would suggest panic, so he continues, finally arriving at his building and then at his door. Still locked. No signs of forced entry. He turns the key and steps in, closing the door behind him and quickly latching the deadbolt, pretending for a moment that it would do any good. Logan pauses on the other side of his door, standing still as he scans what he can see. Everything is exactly as he left it. Every piece of mail, coffee mug, lights left on, radio playing. If there was, or perhaps still is, an intruder, they are not here for sensitive site exploitation. Depending on the kind of message this hypothetical assassin was ordered to send, they might have dusted a nerve agent on the handle of his front door or perhaps crafted a bomb strategically placed under his toilet. Logan might predictably die of suicide, just another death in the daily toll of veterans taking their own lives. Or their tactics might be less subtle, culminating in two bullets to the chest and one in the head. But for right now, Logan remains alive, and he intends to stay that way.

Walking into his kitchen, Logan grabs a full beer from the fridge, twists off the bottle cap, and begins to chug. He then grabs two empty beer bottles from his kitchen countertop. Carrying them to his front door, he methodically stacks the bottles on top of each other directly in front of the door. He continues to chug the new bottle, finishing it quickly and then transporting it to another door at the back of his apartment leading out to a patio. He checks the deadbolt and then rests the empty bottle against the door. Logan then moves into his bedroom and pulls four books off the bookshelf. Resting in the now empty space on the shelf against the wall is a black 9mm handgun, his Beretta, his weapon of choice. He pulls out a thick book on the other side of the shelf, *War and Peace*—a little on the nose, but that is his humor—revealing a stack of loaded magazines. Fifteen rounds, ready to go, safety off. He begins to methodically clear the remaining rooms of his apartment. Two bathrooms and a second bedroom. Handgun raised, firing position, he checks the corners first. Behind the shower curtains. In the closets. All clear.

Logan walks back into the kitchen, opens the fridge, and grabs another beer. Bottle open, he takes a swig. This bottle serves no tactical purpose other than to calm his nerves. He attempts to slow his breathing to a controlled inhale and exhale. Standing in the kitchen for the moment, beer in one hand, handgun in the other, he fixes a cold gaze upon the faded off-white kitchen wall. He ponders his next move and begins to ask himself the pertinent questions. Is there any chance Ivanov's death has nothing to do with Logan's work with the FBI? Unlikely. Besides, it would only be to his great folly to treat a coincidence as such anyway. No, his life will be different now, from this moment forward.

Returning to the present, he glances up to a cabinet above him to the right. He pauses and wishes he could refrain, knowing that some impulse-driven primitive component to his psyche is craving a more profound chemical fix. Logan opens the cabinet and pulls out a pill bottle. Ambien. Of what use would he be to himself, lying awake all night, gripping a gun and homing in on every drip of the faucet and distant city sirens? He pops the lid off and takes a pill, washing it down with a swig of beer.

Thirty minutes later, time becomes distorted. A fully clothed Logan is asleep and sprawled out on top of his bed covers, boots still on. Empty beer bottles sit on the nightstand, while the loaded gun rests next to him in bed in its own state of slumber. The lights are all on in the house. Silence permeates throughout, aside from the occasional whir of Logan's breathing. The sleeping Logan stirs and mumbles audibly, deep in sleep and lost in a violent inescapable dream:

He sees a hotel room in Dupont Circle, Washington, DC. Abnormally bright sunlight shines through the edges of a long curtain pulled closed over the window of the swanky hotel room, casting the entire room in shades of a surreal afternoon glow. Mikhail Ivanov, with skin slightly pale, sits on the edge of the hotel bed, legs hanging over, back stiff and upright, wearing the same clothes he wore the day Logan met him on the plane. Ivanov has a solemn look on his face as he stares directly forward, seemingly piercing Logan's soul without an ounce of humanly warmth. He is silent, only staring. Suddenly a black-gloved hand holding a small steel pipe emerges within the dream from just outside of Logan's point of view, slightly above Ivanov's head. In one swift motion, the pipe comes swinging forcefully down, striking the side of Ivanov's head. The thud of the pipe is unnaturally loud and creates a sort of hollow ringing that leaves Logan shaking in his sleep. The dream continues. Ivanov, having been dealt the violent blow, continues to stare straight ahead, locking eyes with Logan. Blood begins to rapidly drip down his expressionless face. The pipe swings again. And again. Blow after blow is struck. With each vicious swing of downward destruction, Ivanov's head and face are crushed inward. Blood is splattering on the crisp white bed, the pearl walls, and the satin curtains, like a dysfunctional art project of the devil himself. Skull fragments and brain tissue become indistinguishable from the bloody mess of Ivanov's face. Blow after blow until he is no longer recognizable. His body slowly begins to tip over sideways, falling awkwardly onto the bed before rolling off completely. The mysterious black-gloved hand with the steel pipe has vanished now, into the storage bin of unconscious projections.

Logan is stirring in bed, trapped in a medication-induced coma and unable to wake from this nightmare. There is a brief stillness to the visions of hotel-room madness, until heavy, faint breathing can be heard from somewhere behind Logan's dream field of vision. He turns behind him and sees nothing. He turns forward again and hears fluid-filled, labored breathing behind him, like the sound of someone whose lungs have filled with blood. Again he turns around, but now he finds the mutilated Afghan male from his perpetually haunting war flashbacks facing him, wearing the same bloodied traditional Pashtun garb from the day of the drone strike. His clothes are burned and in tatters, revealing holes from mortal wounds in his stomach, intestines hanging out and slithering like a den of snakes on an alien planet. His face and limbs remain intact. His eyes, like Ivanov's, are cold and dead, staring straight into the depths of Logan's morality. The quiet sounds of blood dripping and intestines spilling are slightly audible.

Suddenly, the hotel room door bursts open, and Ivanov's wife and two sons come darting into this unholy fever dream. Paulina, Leo, and Alexander seem neither aghast nor confused at the horror scene in front of them. To Logan's surprise, they do not rush to the slumped-over body of their father and husband. Instead, they swiftly move to the mutilated body of the Afghan male. Leo, with his small, bare hands, begins to pick up the intestines while Paulina directs him to pack the spilled insides back into the mortal wound. She then instructs her boys to grab the feet, while she places her hands under the arms of the motionless body. Collectively they drag the body out of the room and out of sight, never once uttering a word to Logan as the apparition or observer of the grotesque and the morbid.

A voice in the dream calls out from behind Logan. Muffled, with an echo, like someone calling out from the opposite end of a long tunnel. Logan turns back around, expecting to see the body of Ivanov still slumped over on the floor. Instead, Logan sees Brock, sitting upright on the bed, where Ivanov had been moments before. The blood and the violence have vanished. Brock is saying something, mouth moving, but his voice remains muffled. Logan attempts to make sense of the words but struggles to understand them. Brock stares at Logan, mouth continuing to move. Slowly, repeatedly, the words begin to emerge.

"Are you a patriot?" asks Brock in a muffled tone.

"What?" Logan responds.

"Are you a patriot?" Brock asks again, with slightly less obfuscation. He repeats once more, fully audible now. "Are you a patriot?"

Suddenly, the clanking sound of bottles falling interrupts Logan's nightmare, saving him from this feverish hell as he jolts awake, bolting upright in bed and immediately grabbing the gun next to him. The beer bottles on his nightstand remain intact. What he heard, or at least what he thinks he heard, came from the front door, without subsequent sound. From his bed, the delirious Logan aims his gun at the doorway to his room. The door is locked, but he fully expects it to be kicked in. A moment passes and nothing happens. Logan struggles to separate dream from wakefulness. He hops out of bed, weapon drawn and boots on his feet, shuffling toward the bedroom doorway. Whatever moves about on the other side of this door is something Logan must kill. He has no time to consider prison or tending to a gunshot wound of his own. Shoot first in this scenario, he tells himself. The questions he could ask later would be irrelevant anyway when the coroner was declaring his death a suicide. He prefers to survive, at least long enough to write his own narrative.

Logan unlocks his bedroom door and swings it open, taking a step back and to the side in case something vicious comes charging in. Silence. No flashlights, no shouts, no whispers.

He moves methodically into the hallway, finger on the trigger, clearing his corners, eventually arriving at the front door to find the empty beer bottles tipped over. He pauses, listens for the slightest sound on the other side of the door. Nothing. The deadbolt remains locked, but as far as he is concerned, his fate is tied to empty bottles. He is drowsy, confused, and not quite sure if his dream has really ended. The apartment, and Logan within it, is silent for two minutes that feel like two weeks. And then, disrupting the tense but silent state, is the jarring sound of Logan's cell phone ringing from back in his bedroom. With considerable trepidation, he does not yet move, imagining a sequence of events in which his apartment blows up the moment he answers. The phone stops ringing briefly, and then starts up again. Logan moves into his room, gun in hand, and grabs the phone. Unknown caller. He answers with a simple "Hello."

"Did you tell anybody?" asks the voice of Brock on the other end of the line.

"What? This is all so fucked, man," replies Logan.

"Did you fucking tell anybody about your work with us? About Ivanov? About any of it?"

"No, no, I didn't say anything," responds Logan. "I wouldn't. Ever. I'm on the fucking news, man. I watched a video of me on TV with Ivanov."

Logan wonders where Brock is located during this call. Is he alone somewhere, in a state of panic over an operation gone south? Is he in a room full of a dozen other agents, all trying to collectively figure out how to properly unfuck themselves? What was Logan to any of this? Someone expendable, or a loose end?

Brock responds and attempts to put Logan's mind at ease. "Listen, we're gonna take care of it. We'll give them a different suspect. Nobody knows your name, so you should be safe, as long as you don't talk, keep a low profile, stay out of trouble."

"How did this happen?" Logan asks.

"Well somebody talked. Somebody knows that we got to Ivanov."

"Wait," responds Logan. "Did you…get to Ivanov?"

Logan fails to find the answer to the question that he desperately seeks, as the call abruptly ends with a click. Brock has hung up, leaving Logan wholly dissatisfied, with a mind no more at ease than before his handler's reassurances. Unwilling to accept such abstraction, Logan immediately attempts to call Brock at the number he had previously been given. An automated voice answers.

"We're sorry, you have reached a number that has been disconnected or is no longer—"

Logan hangs up. He is beginning to feel like a mouse being battered by a Machiavellian cat, looming large and giving him hope when he has none, taking it away when hope returns. Each time he is told not to worry, he only worries more. It is not delusion that makes him paranoid. It is ambiguity.

CHAPTER 12

Keeping a low profile is something Logan can handle, but the ruminating is driving him mad. He was asked to get close to a target. He was successful. That target is now dead. A wife without a husband. Sons without a father. After eleven days of keeping his head down, these thoughts have grown into a forest of twisted tree limbs occupying the most coveted acreage of his conscious mind. He lives in a state of hypervigilance, wondering when a door will get kicked in or a bullet will find its way to his skull. He sits with his back to the wall, facing the door, whenever and wherever he could. Such is the case in the booth he occupies in a casual DC restaurant at midday, with his friend John sitting across from him, blabbering about politics that seem largely insignificant to Logan's current troubles. Baskets of fish and chips sit in front of both men, along with the requisite beers. Logan wears a hat pulled low and glasses he wouldn't normally wear in public. His facial hair is scruffy and helps him to slightly contort the lines of his cheeks and jaw. He leaves his phone at home.

"I mean it's a fucking joke, honestly," states John, largely speaking to himself and oblivious that Logan's mind is elsewhere. "The whole thing has made a mockery of our political system. And the Libertarians? This is who they fucking choose? It's like you said a couple months ago at the bar..."

Logan is in no mood to discuss politics, and John's complaints about political classes are merely background music to the troubles of his mind. But suddenly, something John says catches Logan's attention, bringing him back to the present moment. John continues speaking as Logan homes in on a particular choice of words.

"...they only fucking care about getting a big enough percentage of the vote that would be decisive if those votes had swung one way or the other."

Logan interrupts, asking, "What did you say? About the bar? That was a couple of months ago, right? We were drunk; it was more than a disdain for modern politics. What else happened that night?"

"Yeah man," responds John. "It was that night we got fucked up over on U Street. You were sloppy. Well, OK, we were both sloppy. Remember that, on the walk back though? You were emotional, talking about the war shit?"

Logan's tone quickly becomes more animated, more urgent. He has shifted from a zoned-out posture into an outright intense stare, leaving John confused in the moment.

"You said I was really drunk that night? I think the next day you told me I couldn't stop talking about war, right? What else did I tell you? What about the more recent past? Did I say anything? Anything about what I've been up to outside of school? This is important. Think back."

"What do you mean, dude? You talked about the Christie chick, about being burned out from classes—"

"No!" shouts Logan, cutting John off rudely, aggressively. "I told you something, didn't I! About that other shit, the shit that Alex got me involved in?"

John, ordinarily never one to be conscientious, looks around the restaurant in embarrassment, as if hoping to find the eyes of fellow nearby diners and apologize on behalf of his friend. He lowers his voice now and responds.

"Logan, calm down dude. Are you talking about the FBI stuff? I mean, you told me you were helping them out sometimes, that you felt like maybe it would be good for you to be catching bad guys again. I don't know dude, Alex asked me to get involved in the same shit, but why would I? I don't want to talk about war when we drink, man. I don't want to cry over this shit."

Logan places both hands on the table and elevates himself up off the booth slightly. He should care about the setting. He should care about his friend. But he is a madman, eyes wide and paranoid. With misplaced priorities and emotions getting in the way, he is failing quickly at maintaining a low profile.

"Who did you tell?" he shouts. "Who the fuck did you tell?"

"What?" asks an incredulous John. "I don't tell anybody about our conversations, man. Why would you—"

Logan interrupts once again.

"Who did you fucking tell? Answer me!"

"You're freaking me out dude!" responds an anxious John. "Fuck this! This is bullshit. I gotta leave, man. You gotta get some fucking help!"

John abruptly stands up, throws some money down on the table, and storms out of the restaurant. Most of the other diners are now staring at Logan, judging and whispering among themselves. What is all of this costing him? To drive others away, to lose the ground beneath his feet. Is he detached from reality? Or has his reality become so surreal that the world is detached from him? Logan sits back down in the booth, picks up his beer, and attempts to calmly drink. He has drifted into an abyss and wonders if he might ever find land again.

* * *

Logan has missed enough classes to the point where his peers, and his professors, have begun to notice. Even the quiet ones cannot fade away where a doctorate, funding, and student loans are concerned. Back on the campus, Logan's classmates are listening to a professor in her seventies, wearing a tweed blazer and glasses, attempt to wrap up a lecture at the pace of something glacial. Christie, sitting near the back of the classroom, is more concerned about the empty desk sitting next to her than she is the quips of the elderly academic. She is surrounded by about ten other students seated in desks as the professor drones on.

"Alright, well as promised, I'm letting you out early. Maybe only two minutes early, but I kept my promise!" proclaims the professor, laughing as if she's told a joke that only she finds funny. She continues, "So next week I'd like to have everyone's proposal for your research topics. The following week, as a reminder, I'll be asking for your references. Alright, that's it, have a great weekend!"

The other students stand to collect their belongings and make for the exits in haste, as if the longer they stick around, the greater the probability that they'll get pulled into some academic project or special request from a program head. Christie, meanwhile, stares at the empty desk. A look of concern occupies her face as she slowly stands and gathers her laptop and bag, heading for the exterior of the classroom building. It's afternoon in Washington, DC, as she emerges. The usual sounds of honking horns and sirens can be heard all around, like an orchestra playing to her emotions. She pulls her cell phone out of her pocket, dials a number, and holds the phone up to her mouth, as if she already knows that the call will result in a message being left rather than a conversation being had.

"Hey Logan, it's Christie," she speaks into the phone. "Look, I get that maybe you're just not in a place in your life for a relationship. You did try to warn me, after all. And if we're not going to talk anymore for whatever reason, it's fine. But you haven't been to class all week and I heard you canceled all your clinic appointments for the week too. I'm worried about you. I probably shouldn't be, but I just want to know you're OK. Can we please talk? Just call me, please."

She is a good girl, a Catholic girl, a saint for all seasons. Logan had once attempted to avoid her, rather poorly, back when they were new classmates, fearing that he might corrupt some innocence that the cynical war veteran in him wanted to loathe, an innocence that he knew might pull him back from teetering on an edge that he pretended to prefer. But it all seems so dramatic to him now. Logan is grateful to have been such an asshole as to spare her from all of this, but he is also grateful that somehow she still cares enough about him to be worried. He wants to feel her touch, to be comforted and reminded that life doesn't have to be this way. But he is too ashamed to crawl out of the pit of paranoia and helplessness that he has found himself in, and as such he is terrified that Christie will come knocking on his door. He will not answer for her or anyone, knowing that his door will not be opening unless a SWAT team is kicking it in. In the meantime, his blinds stay closed and the sunlight is kept out. He sits shirtless on the couch in the living room of his apartment, unshaven and haggard. He is trained to survive, to evade, to stay strong in the face of torture, but existing in a perpetual state of such a purgatory is not a skill that he had learned in survival school. He is at once both servant and enemy of the state, and his fate feels locked in a Gordian knot that leaves him too paralyzed to know how to begin or which direction to pull.

His coffee table is littered with empty beer cans and bottles of prescription pills. His sleep is purely medication induced, but even that will run out eventually. He keeps the TV on and a film plays but he can't watch. Periodically, he checks all the locks in his home. The windows, the doors, the safety of his Beretta. A confusing paradox has established itself within his ever-hypervigilant mind. He is prepared to do whatever he must to survive, and yet he is increasingly desperate for an ending. He is filled with rage toward others, but he blames himself for the foolish errors of his own loyalty. He tells himself that a vicious fate will befall any man who attempts to barge through his door, but he remains terrified of the sound of squirrels on his rooftop. This psychological superposition, an innate drive to live, and a desperate desire to die, is leaving him exhausted. The external threats are numerous, but the internal foe is the most formidable of all. A voice has crept in, telling him that there is only one way out of this predicament, that there is one inevitable conclusion, the ultimate disillusionment. He was the purveyor of death, of pain, of burden. And now he must atone for all those sins.

Absolution could become the focal point of all his rumination. He asks himself if he is deserving of it, and typically the answer is no, not now and not ever. He is a transitional object, a vessel that carries death from point A to point B on behalf of dubious forces. He is nobody's hero, nobody's saint, nobody's martyr. His self-pity is profound and debilitating enough to push him downhill and watch him roll. He hates himself for hating himself, for contemplating a permanent stillness, for wishing he knew how to quit. He is told so often that twenty-two veterans a day are committing suicide. He wonders how many of these deaths are the result of a moral injury, of a clash between morals and ideals, between humanity and depravity. Logan wonders how many of these veterans were consciously thinking in their final moments about becoming the newest members of this morbid club, the club of twenty-two. Was it enough to believe your death would be used to justify grant funding that someday might be used to justify more?

During these darkest hours, he tries to remember the letters and drawings he received while deployed to Iraq from American school children. An elementary school somewhere sent him a box of letters to be distributed to his squadron. He passed them around and kept a few for himself. They wrote about their superpowers, their pet dogs, their teachers. One kid simply wrote that he was a "vampire" and nothing more. Logan laughed for days afterward. Mostly, though, the letters referred to Logan and his fellow airmen as "heroes" and said they were going to be "Army men" just like them. They wrote about "freedom" and drew American flags. They expressed gratitude and said thank you for serving and keeping them safe. Logan cried, silently, away from everyone as he read through them, leaning against a concrete pillar to stop the incoming mortar rounds. It was a strange juxtaposition out there in the desert. Staring through an infrared lens, he had watched helplessly as aid workers were beheaded. He had seen barbarians fornicating with dogs, explosions ripping through hotels, and terrorists be given safe passage on escape routes merely because they made last-minute deals with Western governments and were thus able to avoid ever having to pay for their atrocities. This world was no place for heroes. But there was some solace in these letters for Logan, some solace in knowing that something back home could retain its innocence for now, without being corrupted by the reality that war was rarely ever so black-and-white. Perhaps Logan even yearned for a return to those days himself, when he still believed that service and sacrifice could rise above the whims of Washington.

And now, alone and disheartened as never before, those letters provide the last remaining ounce of hope he has left. He imagines himself as a young schoolboy at the age of six, sitting around a tiny table in a tiny chair as the teacher moved around the room in a circle, asking each of the kids what they wanted to be when they grew up. Little Johnny was going to be an astronaut. Little Suzie was going to be a pop star. Little Molly was going to race horses. Little Logan Callahan was going to become an expert in getting close to a target and then sticking around long enough to help facilitate their very violent death. Little Bobby was going to become the president, and so on.

In truth, it is hard for Logan to recall anything he was ever going to be, other than what he is right now. Every hand he had been dealt and every card he had chosen to play somehow led to him being suicidal and broken in his living room, a man whose loyalties could so readily be exploited, a man who tortures himself with a hyperfixation on the consequences of his own actions. His personality, he feels, had perhaps become too abrasive to the point where he pushed away the shoulders he might have wished to lean on, while his guilt left him vulnerable to the mercy of those who would use military veterans as a means to an end.

Logan's phone rests on the edge of the coffee table. He reaches with a frustrated sigh and unlocks it, pressing the last number dialed on his recent calls. The same number had been dialed twenty-seven times previously. This is the last number that Brock had called him with, and thus, this is the number he repeatedly dials, hoping illogically that at some point, he might experience a different result. The automated voice, however, rejects him yet again, just as it has all twenty-seven times prior.

"We're sorry, you have reached a number that has been disconnected—"

He hangs up and dials again.

"We're sorry, you have reached a number that has been disconnected or is no longer—"

He tosses the phone angrily back onto the coffee table, only for it to ring the moment it lands. For a split second, he is relieved, imagining Brock will tell him everything is safe now. Alas, the call is from Christie. She leaves him the concerned voicemail, which only makes him feel more guilty. His phone rings twice more. Once from the Old Man, his mentor, who leaves Logan a message in his long, meandering, and frail voice.

"Hi Logan. I haven't spoken to you in a while and wanted to check in on our research project. I have a suggestion regarding a grant proposal. But we'll need to submit soon. Let me know if this is something you can do. We should really consider meeting soon at my office. It really has been too long since I heard from you. I would prefer that you keep me updated on the project. Also, I had a conversation with some colleagues recently that I think would be of interest to you. Give me a call back."

The research seems largely irrelevant to Logan at the moment, and he wonders if he will ever call the Old Man back again.

The next and final call is devastating. This is John calling to deliver news that Logan had never anticipated receiving. Logan is torn about answering, but he has regrets about pushing John away and hopes this might be the beginning of his opportunity to make amends. But John is calling for a different matter entirely.

"Hello?" answers Logan.

"Logan, it's John. It's about Alex."

"What about him?"

"He's dead."

"What? What do you mean?"

"I mean he's dead," responds John. His voice cracks, and Logan can tell he is struggling to keep it together. "It was suicide, man. He shot himself. It's fucked up…I don't know, dude…It's fucked up."

"Holy shit, man," responds Logan. "All the dude ever did was laugh and smile and crack jokes."

"Yeah well, you're the expert," John answers, his voice now a combination of anger, sadness, and confusion.

"Did he leave a note? I mean, what the hell happened?" asks Logan. The gravity of losing his military friend was starting to set in now.

"All I know is that the funeral is on Monday."

* * *

The cemetery is about an hour outside of Washington, DC. The weather on that particular Monday is bright and sunny, far more pleasant than it has any right to be. It almost seems cruel. Alex could be annoyingly lighthearted, but his suicide should have been the extinguishment of anything warm, at least for a little while. At the funeral, his brother speaks, which Logan and John find ironic because Alex often hinted at some level of estrangement between the two. There is a priest in attendance as well, but Alex had grown deeply suspicious of his family's Catholicism long before the war and even more so after. Perhaps his death had been voluntary, but the narrative that followed is not. Suddenly, everyone had been his best friend. Maybe this is how people grapple with the aftermath of a loved one's suicide, by desperately needing to believe they did all they could.

There are details Logan wants but will never receive. It doesn't feel right to ask the family. Not now, anyway. He knows the cause of death is a bullet wound to the brain. Alex rented a shitty house somewhere near the college he was attending. If you stood in his living room, you could peer through holes in the floor and stare directly into the basement. When he had moved in, there was a bird's nest in a kitchen light fixture. The appliances rarely worked, but he didn't need much. He ate rice and went to class. Sometimes, he would sleep in his truck anyway. In spite of the disrepair of the home, he was always rather fond of his landlord. And thus, he didn't take his life inside the house. He walked to the edge of his small yard and stood alongside a sidewalk that ran parallel to a fairly busy road. It seemed as though he wanted the whole world to know that he alone took responsibility for pulling that trigger.

When the artist Vincent van Gogh shot himself, he did so in the chest. This was attempted suicide, but he didn't die immediately from the bullet. It was the sepsis from the wound that finally killed him days later. On his deathbed, van Gogh allegedly muttered the words, "The sadness will last forever." It wasn't despair that made him suicidal. It was his belief that the despair would never end. He could no longer convince himself that every night would give way to a sunrise.

On the day his friend was buried, Logan cannot help but wonder what had felt so permanent and unbearable for Alex that he could only see one way out. Alex probably had a multitude of demons like the rest of them. Some of which Logan knows all too well. They were men haunted by what they had done and by what they could not stop doing.

Logan and John walk through the cemetery together afterward. That is when Logan finally lets the tears hit, when nobody but John is looking.

"He was so upbeat. What the hell happened?" asks John.

"It's not like you and I never think about it, man. He just beat us to it," replies Logan.

"Have you been thinking about it?" John asks.

Logan answers, "I've been in a dark place, brother. You know that. But then I come here today, and look into the eyes of Alex's mom. She looks like a part of her soul was buried down there with her son. And then we listen to people who didn't really know him talking about memories that hardly happened, and I just, I don't want any of that."

There is a long, contemplative pause as both men continue walking quietly through the cemetery. Logan breaks the silence.

"Listen, man, I'm sorry about the other night. You didn't deserve any of that. Between you, Alex, and myself, you were the only one with enough common sense to say no when the IC tried pulling us back in. I don't know why I always have to try and prove myself. But that's my shit, not yours. I'm sorry, man."

"It's alright, dude. I just want you to be able to enjoy your life, you know?"

* * *

Days later, Logan manages to fully reemerge into the world, if only to say his goodbyes. There will be no follow-up call from Brock. He will never receive an all clear or a thank you for his service once again as a wayward patriot searching for approval. No bullet will yet arrive for him, at least not by his own volition. He will have to live with the unsteady feeling that his identity will forever be intricately linked to the tragedies of others, and that his awareness of proximity to this violence is itself his own tragedy to bear. He will sit with his back to the wall of every restaurant. He will struggle to sleep without pills or booze. Others will find him distant, quiet, but occasionally disarmingly charming. He will silently question the intentions of others. He will assume his days are numbered. But he will choose to live. And for now, that promise to himself is enough.

He mentions none of this, of course, as he sits on the couch in the Old Man's home office in Bethesda. Logan looks fairly put together, although he is letting his hair grow out and his beard grow longer. Nothing in his appearance suggests a man who had recently been through an emotional spiral of catastrophizing and paranoia. He sips on a cup of coffee-flavored gasoline, pretending to enjoy the aroma of stale beans as the porcelain and tribal masks look down upon him. The Old Man sits across from him with a cup of coffee of his own, his pudgy body slumped into a chair that was probably an antique ten years prior. For a brief moment, both men are quiet. The Old Man seems particularly tired, lost in thoughts of his own. Logan looks up at him and prepares to ask a question. He hesitates, though, and the Old Man can sense this.

"A penny for your thoughts?" asks the Old Man.

"Well, I suppose I was curious," Logan begins to ask. "You spent a long time in the intelligence community...How did you ever learn to trust people in your life?

"Oh, well, that's simple," answers the Old Man without pause. "I didn't."

He takes a moment, reflects, and smiles to himself as if there's satisfaction in his answer. He continues. "There really is nothing more taxing on the human psyche than the burden of knowledge. An old friend of mine once said, 'A man who has the tools to light up the darkest of corners is also the first to know what's been kept hiding.' It's hard, maybe impossible, to trust anyone once you become that man."

He has always liked to regale Logan with stories of dictators who had pushed their luck one too many times. The Old Man was personally responsible for a dozen coup attempts, some of which were actually successful. But when an overthrow would go awry and a more immediate fix was needed, sometimes a difficult foreign leader might mysteriously experience an untimely death on a toilet or sadly encounter a sudden mechanical error on a helicopter ride. Sometimes a country needed to be transformed and a dictator might become a casualty of that transformation. Sometimes a country needed to remain the same, and leadership had to go in order to maintain the status quo. But the Old Man was never going to be the one planting a bomb or sifting through its aftermath. Maybe killing should not be so compartmentalized. Maybe every death should be worn around the neck, carried like a weight, eventually dragging the owner down when it all becomes too heavy.

The Old Man had never served in the military. He knew the spy game well, but he avoided getting his own hands dirty. He belonged to the old guard, the Yale and Georgetown graduates who were motivated less by American exceptionalism and more by their own. They were valuable assets who could win a geopolitical chess match from afar but would be too much of a liability in a dark alley at night.

Logan still respects him immensely, but he now realizes, finally, that he wants nothing to do with the duplicity of it all. The game has grown so big and limitless, and now there are too many players playing games within games within games, to the point that the original rules have become obfuscated behind the veil of some abstract version of loyalty. Nobody really knows who they were fighting or why anymore, other than the tired old bumper-sticker slogans about freedom and democracy and America. The CIA hides assets from the FBI and the FBI chases the Agency's assets at home and abroad, while the NSA watches it all unfold in silence. Enemies are created to justify spending, which is then used to justify bigger budgets, creating a balloon that is enriching for some and fatal for others.

Meanwhile, Ivanov is dead and Logan will be too if he doesn't remove himself from the equation on terms that keep him above ground. There are real enemies out there, burning the flag on battlefields and city sidewalks. But trying to fight a war without faith in the man next to you is a futile effort. Logan wanted an honest brotherhood but ended up as a lone wolf, deep in a forest of dead leaves and gray skies. If it is shelter he is seeking, he won't find it inside the beltway of Washington, DC.

"You know, that reminds me," continues the Old Man. "I was talking to some friends at my old employer. They suggested you give them a call. They'd like to talk to you about a position."

"Thank you," replies Logan. "But I think, perhaps, those days are behind me now."

"Oh, well, that's a shame. They can always use a man like you."

CHAPTER 13

One year later

Stretches of Little Goose Creek during the colder months sometimes amount to nothing more than a trickle. But when the weather warms and the snow in the Big Horns melts, Little Goose Creek flows mightily enough to provide the perfect ambient noise for sleeping. At the base of the Big Horn Mountains, along the bank of that creek, stands a small cabin, approximately six hundred square feet in size, built by a family of Mennonites fifty years prior. The same family still owns the cabin, but for a decade now, they have rented it out to tenants in need of a cheap home and a minimalist lifestyle somewhere far off the beaten path. Often, these tenants are ranch hands and cowboys. They stick around for about six months until the work dries up and then they move on. Occasionally, they get in trouble with the law and the lease ends earlier. There was a girl from Chicago once, a yoga teacher, who had moved in with excitement and moved out three months later in defeat. The quiet, rugged living demands a certain temperament for penance and tends to be unforgiving in its absence.

The adolescent kids in the Mennonite family keep a close eye on the renters. Not because they are distrusting, but because neighbors tend to be few and far between, and being curious is what counts for entertainment in these parts. There are largely two types of people living in this region of Wyoming: Those who were born and raised here and never had any intention of going anywhere else, and those who moved here from elsewhere in the country specifically because they wanted to be left the hell alone.

The current tenant of the Mennonite cabin of Little Goose Creek certainly falls within the latter category. While he is friendly and respectful to his landlords, he is perhaps the most mysterious tenant the family has ever experienced. They have never rented to a psychologist before, and this one wears tweed blazers and drives a dirty truck. He is young and attractive, with a quiet intensity that some find perplexing. About a month after he arrived, he came home one evening with a puppy, a black mutt that resembled an Australian Shepherd, which he named "Raskol," and said was short for "Raskolnikov," a reference that nobody but him seems to understand or appreciate. On late Friday afternoons, he arrives home with a pizza and a six pack of beer. On Saturdays, he emerges from the cabin wearing a large backcountry hiking pack with a tent poking out and a bear cannister attached with a carabiner that swings as he walks. He wears a handgun around his waist, a can of bear spray and a large knife at his hip, military-style hiking boots laced up with his pants tucked in, and a neatly wound bundle of 550 cord readily accessible from the exterior of his pack. He hikes up toward the mountains and isn't seen for the remainder of the weekend.

The Mennonite family keeps a large herd of goats on their land near the cabin. A middle child once left the gate open on a Wednesday, and fifteen goats took it upon themselves to wander. They were smart animals, but a little too bold for their own good. The mysterious tenant, the psychologist, arrived home in his truck that day and immediately helped the family corral the goats. He wore his tweed blazer, and his puppy followed by his side. Few words were spoken, and fourteen goats in total were found and returned. The last, the fifteenth goat, was less fortunate. Mountain lions were common in the area, and one had taken advantage of a stray goat as evidenced by blood droplets and tracks that led deeper into the family's land. The Mennonite father and his eldest son invited the tenant to accompany them in tracking down the mountain lion. He was the first to spot the beast and alert the father, who raised his rifle, pulled the trigger, and brought the animal down. The tenant helped load the body of the mountain lion onto a sled attached to the back of the father's ATV. He asked no questions and said very little. Two weeks later, the tenant found a box outside the front door of his cabin with a note attached that read, "Logan—Thank you for your help. This is for you. With gratitude." Logan opened the box to find the pelt of a mountain lion. This was the life he needed.

There are other cabins around, mostly individuals, some families. Many are homesteaders, growing their own crops, working at self-sustainability, maintaining flocks of free-range chickens, which Logan sometimes finds roaming around his yard. He never minds any of it. The chickens help to keep the insects away, which are already fairly minimal due to the elevation. He takes pleasure in watching Raskol chase these yardbirds around, although he is never quite sure what would happen if his dog ever actually manages to catch one. The homesteaders sometimes bring him free eggs, for which he is grateful. He is a mystery to them as well.

The town, to the extent that there is one, stands on the opposite side of Little Goose Creek from Logan's cabin. The post office, the little restaurant, the dusty old bar, they are all exactly how Logan had expected, exactly how he had wanted them to be. At the post office, Raskol tends to receive more mail than Logan does, an indication of a proud and spoiled dog. At the restaurant, Logan always orders a steak with a side of okra and a tall pint of whatever beer is available at the time. The food is consistently dry but there is comfort in the predictability. Most often, though, if Logan is spotted in town, walking down that gravel main street, he is heading to his real home away from home, a barstool inside The Holdfast Saloon. Logan's journey to his preferred bar, the only bar, requires nothing more than a half-mile walk. There is an old, rusty footbridge that was erected over the creek at some distant point in history, allowing the more remote residents of this remote town easy access to the fulfillment of all their postal, sustenance, and bibation needs. Logan enjoys this walk over the bridge and through the town. There are butterflies, pollinating bees, and, on at least two occasions, black bears that quickly scamper off.

There is a neon sign that once used to light up the exterior of The Holdfast Saloon, but the sign stopped working twenty years ago, and nobody cared enough to fix it. The interior of the bar is only slightly bigger than Logan's cabin and never comes close to being filled to capacity. There are two tables, seven barstools, one pool table, and a malfunctioning jukebox. The walls are adorned with framed newspaper clippings and pictures from the local rodeo. Fifty years' worth of cigarette smoke created a heavy stench that permeates throughout the walls and the décor. There were signs that say "No Smoking," but they are dismissed merely as a formality. On Friday nights, the bartender is a blonde siren named Nicky who dresses provocatively and earns tips with the flash of a smile. Logan tends to stay away on Friday nights. He prefers to throw out tips that are commensurate with the pour and not the eyelashes. He also has a history with Nicky. There is always a history. On all other nights, though, there is a different bartender, Linda, who functions as the sole employee. She pours strong drinks, hastily cleans the establishment, and kicks out troublemakers, all with nary a smile or an ounce of conviviality. If someone tells her they're hungry, she'll offer a pickled egg that has been in a jar behind the bar since 1982. Few ever dare to take her up on the offer. Logan estimates Linda's age to be somewhere around sixty, plus or minus a decade because it's possible she was simply born cantankerous. Linda has auburn-gray hair and speaks with a firm and raspy voice that Logan sometimes finds strangely gentle. She likes Logan and finds his demeanor to be tolerable, if not a little odd. Theirs is a symbiotic relationship fueled by sarcasm and dry wit. Logan enjoys finding out how often he can elicit an eyeroll from Linda. She enjoys sharing a drink with him from behind the bar.

Logan has been working as a therapist at a Veterans Affairs Medical Center. The work is heavy and the days are long. Linda has become his saving grace, a savior of the pour. On this particular Thursday, Logan arrives home from work, parks his truck, lets his puppy outside, and then immediately makes his way to The Holdfast Saloon. The place is nearly empty, with the exception of the town drunk sitting in the corner, a man whom Logan has long referred to as "Fred," although he can never quite remember if that is indeed this gentleman's real name. Linda will never admit it, but she is happy to see Logan when he walks through the door, tweed blazer and all.

"The usual?" she asks him.

"Yes ma'am. I'm thirsty, Linda. Very thirsty."

She pours a beer for him and places it down on the bar as he prepares to grab a seat. She has her own half-full pint of beer behind the bar.

"You want to take that jacket off, kid?" she asks. "You're making me hot just looking at you."

"I do that to a lot of women, Linda."

"Oh Lord."

She rolls her eyes, and Logan is pleased with himself. Behind her above the bar is a TV that Linda keeps set on cable news. Anyone showing up to The Holdfast Saloon with the intention of watching a sports game will be sorely disappointed to learn that Linda needs her news more than you need your game. Logan glances up at the TV to hear a Southern senator attempt to make the case for launching a preemptive military strike on a country in the Middle East.

"Seems like they want another war," Linda remarks.

Logan responds, "You know Linda, maybe war was never meant to be something we perpetually threaten, but rather something we do when we have to do it. And something we prepare for in the meantime. These clowns pound their fists on the pulpit and scream about protecting democracy in places where people are more worried about whether they'll have access to clean drinking water and women have to worry about mutilation or getting thrown in a van for wearing the wrong outfit."

"You must be real fun at parties, huh?" asks Linda. She finds a certain pleasure in getting him riled up.

Logan laughs and replies, "Linda, this is the only party I need right here." He takes a swig of beer and continues. "I can promise you it won't be their brothers and sons and daughters who are left doing the fighting to justify their photo ops. While people like you and I, Linda, might be scum to the elitists living in that bubble, we are the scum they'd need to save a nation they hate."

"Speak for yourself, Captain America," she replies with her dry wit. "I'd be lucky if I could run twenty feet. You don't want to see these old bones on the battlefield."

"Somebody has to serve drinks in hell, Linda," he replies, as Linda laughs and walks away to check on Fred.

Next to the front entrance of the bar is a large window with an incredible view of the Big Horn Mountains looming in the distance. Logan turns his gaze away from the TV to peer out the window, to get lost in the view of an Edward Hopper landscape. He smiles as if the clean mountain air has filled his lungs for a brief moment, as if he's on top of the mountain instead of on top of the barstool. His moment of meditation is disrupted with an announcement on the TV of a breaking news story. Logan turns to watch the TV just as Linda returns to do the same. A news anchor, wearing a suit so glossy and expensive that it looks cheap, strikes an overly serious tone in an attempt to convince the audience they're about to hear something that all the pundits hope will create a level of catastrophic tumult for years to come. The news anchor reports:

"Folks, we now have breaking news to report. We have just learned from sources in DC that the former Director of the Federal Bureau of Investigation, the FBI, is going to be appointed as special counsel to oversee the special investigation into alleged Russian interference in the 2016 election, and to investigate possible collusion between President Donald Trump and the Russian government. This is a huge news story coming out of DC, folks."

Linda, from behind the bar, shakes her head and appears annoyed. She shifts closer toward Logan.

"What do you think about all this?" she asks Logan. "Seems like DC ain't nothing but a bunch of swamp creatures living on a hill, looking down at the rest of us, right kid?"

A faint smile emerges on Logan's face. He appears strangely at peace, as if some form of radical acceptance has swept over him, creating a profound congruency between affect and mood.

"That city, Linda?" says Logan. "It's not a hill. It's a mound, built on the bones of disillusioned ambitious Americans who were sold one too many convincing lies about the romanticism of going to Washington and making a difference. And that swamp? It's not a swamp. It's a graveyard. That's where patriots go to be cleansed of all that God-and-country fervor.

It's the land of posturing while the rest of us drown. But not me, Linda, not me. Naw, I got everything I need right here.

Logan picks up his glass of beer and holds it up as if to make a toast to Linda. She picks up her own glass of beer from behind the bar. They clink their glasses together.

Logan adds, "To hopes and dreams, baby."

"To hopes and dreams, kid," she responds.

Logan drinks down the rest of his beer and places the empty beer mug on the bar in front of him. Linda paces herself but seems to delight in the moment.

"You want another beer, sweetie?" she asks him.

"Sure Linda, that would be great."

Linda grabs Logan's empty beer mug and turns to fill it up again. As she sets the full beer back down in front of Logan, his attention shifts back to the TV. The news anchors attempt to maintain their solemnity, but something deeper is masked. Games within games, Logan thinks to himself. He begins to laugh quietly, as if recalling a joke from another time. His gaze shifts back to the full beer in front of him. He grabs the mug and takes a drink.

EPILOGUE

There are five hundred miles between Logan's seat at The Holdfast Saloon and the small skiing town of Breckenridge, Colorado. Five hundred miles due south, over the jagged, steep terrain of Black Tooth Mountain and the gray, rounded quartzite edges of Medicine Bow Peak. Over the cottonwood and rocky mountain junipers. Over the families of black bears, the moose, and the endless numbers of antelope that glide through the tall prairie fields and powdery snow. Near the base of the Tenmile Range and standing at an elevation of just under ten thousand feet, Breckenridge is full of a constant stream of tourists all year round, who take in the splendid mountain views and ample supply of ski slopes. As such, seasonal workers are also common, as are part-time residents who live here only a short portion of the year. It is the kind of town in which everyone can be a stranger, and all strangers are welcomed. It is the perfect town for Mikhail Ivanov. And on this particular late Thursday afternoon, Ivanov is sitting at a table in an outdoor patio of a small café, surrounded by breathtaking views of the Rocky Mountains. He wears a beard now and looks older, refined but weathered. He masks his Russian accent to the best of his ability, but if he ever falters, he tells inquiring minds that he came from Estonia, a country that most Westerners are largely unfamiliar with, and they don't know what they don't know. He is dressed in an expensive fur-lined winter coat, sitting back in a chair, appreciating the views and drinking wine. This establishment is the only establishment he has found in the local area that serves Georgian wine, and thus it has become a personal favorite.

His mood is contemplative yet peaceful. He has found his Colorado, or rather, he has been allowed to find it, and allowed to live within it. The price for this tranquility is his life, or at least the death of the life he used to know. There is no rebirth without sacrifice, without the surgical removal of what once was, without the grief of the old way. He had made a bargain, and a debt is owed. A debt will forever be owed. For the mountain air could easily disappear with rapidity, and they will not soon let him forget this. His handlers can be rather firm in this regard. They should be arriving at any moment. He selected a table with two additional chairs, one for Harry and the other for Brock. They walk in without fanfare, without enthusiasm. Ivanov has never been fond of Harry's demeanor and often finds himself wishing they might express more gratitude, but he keeps this to himself. His handlers are not the sort to respond to constructive criticism, and he holds no cards to offer it. Such is the deal he accepted.

"Well, Mikhail, we've held up our end of the bargain," said Harry. "We kept our promises. Look around you. It doesn't get better than this. As an official Colorado resident, I hope you'll appreciate these views. Remember, they don't have to last forever."

"That's right, Mikhail," adds Brock. "Now it's your turn to keep your promises. As a brand-new American citizen, I believe it's your patriotic duty, even, to keep those promises. Are you a patriot, Mikhail?"

THE END

ACKNOWLEDGMENTS

Thank you to my beautiful wife, Brooke, for your love and patience.

And a special thank you to those individuals who have always supported my writing, my pursuits, and my occasional insanity: Barry, Debbie, Curt, Tharon, Alex, James, and Ben. And thank you to Chad for pushing me out of the way that day.

ABOUT THE AUTHOR

C.L. McGinnis is a cantankerous military veteran, a recovering former member of the intelligence community, and a psychologist residing somewhere in the low country of South Carolina. When he is not writing, he often spends his time thinking about what he's going to write—someday.